BROKEN

BOOK 1

TT KOVE

ARCTIC CIRCLE PRESS

PART I
CHAD

*J*umping my English teacher in the teacher's lounge was a brilliant idea at the time.

He was sitting there, looking at me all concerned but also with a hint of caring, and he was saying something about me needing to be careful.

Careful?

The fuck would I need to be careful for?

I was on top of the world!

On top of the world… and horny.

And he was right there, in all his tall, broad, slightly stubbled glory—and I desired him. I'd never needed anyone before the way I needed him. Lust coursed through me, my cock sprung from limp to hard in a second—and the brilliant idea popped into my mind.

So I jumped him.

It toppled us over, and he grunted in pain as the back of his chair and his head hit the floor.

My knees took the brunt of it too, but I didn't even feel it.

All I felt was his hard body underneath me and his stubble raking my palms as I cupped his face.

And then I mashed our lips together and all other thoughts flew out of my mind.

I'd fancied him for months—ever since the term started and he'd held me back after class to ask if I was doing okay. I'd sported some bruise or another at the time, which had prompted his concern. My infatuation hadn't lessened since, and I'd finally taken proper advantage of it.

"Chad." He pushed against my shoulders, but I wasn't getting distracted from this.

I wanted him and I knew he wanted me. I'd caught him looking at me too many times to count.

"Dion." I pushed his shirt up from his trousers and thrust my hands underneath. His skin was warm and hard, rippling with muscle that wasn't noticeable in his proper, posh clothing style.

I wondered if he dressed more casual at home, or if he was this proper all the time.

The thought flitted through my head and was gone just as quickly.

Dion's hands clenched on my hips.

I was pleased to feel them on me.

Almost as pleased as I was by him now answering my kisses.

I needed to feel more of him. This had to be taken further and it had to happen now, so I wasted no time undoing his trousers and shoving them down.

His cock slapped against his stomach the minute I freed it, already hard and leaking.

"You want me so much." *I* wanted him so much. I'd never wanted anyone the way I wanted him, that was for sure. Everyone else only wanted a bang, but Dion… he cared about me, and I cared about him too, which was why this was so right!

"Chad…" His eyes were half-closed and clouded over with lust. He was gorgeous like that, but I needed to see him come undone.

For me, only for me.

I stood up to chuck my jeans, in which time he managed to sit up as well. "Don't move." I pushed against his chest and dropped into his lap, my bare skin rubbing against the soft fabric of his trousers.

I wanted to feel him skin to skin, but all I really needed at the moment was his cock, and that stood proud and ready.

"Chad, we don't have—"

"We do." I produced a condom and a packet of lube from my discarded jeans.

I didn't hesitate rolling the condom on him once I'd ripped the packet open with my teeth. Lube followed, which I only bothered drizzling over him. I didn't need it, I'd easily take him.

It would be enough.

It was quick and rough and hard and I *loved* it.

I shifted between clawing at him and clinging to him, and his strong arms were a vice around my middle. If not for his grip, I would've tumbled off his lap in my eagerness, but he kept me on course.

His cock was big and wonderful and it stretched me open in a way few had before. I'd been with a considerable amount of men—but few who was as hung as Dion was.

It was *awesome*!

Before I even knew it—before I was ready—it was over.

I'd come all over his chest, ruining his posh shirt, and he'd filled up the condom inside me.

He struggled to draw in a breath, at the same time as he was already softening inside me.

I slid off his lap and stretched out on the floor.

"That," I put as much emphasis on the word as I could, "was amazing!" I'd come hard, judging by the evidence of his ruined shirt, but my cock was still hard and ready. My body was still pumping. "Let's do it again!" I rolled to the side, wanting to ravage him, but this time he stopped me with a hand splayed on my chest.

"Let's not."

"Come on, I know you think it was good too. Evidence speaks for itself." I rubbed my hand over his now soft cock, which was still encased with the semen-filled condom.

"I'm your teacher." He pushed my hand away then grabbed hold of it when I tried to rub his dick again. He squeezed tightly. "This is unethical. It never should've happened. And as it is... I have someone."

"A girlfriend?" I gave him a shrewd look. He clearly wasn't as interested in said girlfriend after giving in to me so quickly. Maybe he should reevaluate his life choices a bit.

Change gears, so to speak.

"A boyfriend, actually." He grimaced as he took off the condom with his free hand.

"He's clearly not giving you everything you need." I leaned in close, my lips brushing his slightly stubbled jaw. "I can give you absolutely everything, Dion."

"I love Jeremy." He had an emphasis on the

word love.

"So? Love… sex… two different things."

"Two different things that still belong together." He let go off my hand, but he'd pulled his pants and trousers up before I could fondle him again.

I lay back down on the floor and stretched out.

I'd been in the teacher's lounge yesterday too, and I'd thought the ceiling had been dull. Dull and white and boring.

What had I been on about?

It was *lovely*!

The lights gave it a yellow sort of glow and yellow was a happy colour.

It was a happy ceiling.

It *glowed*.

"Chad? Chad!"

I jerked my head around.

Dion stood now, his hands smoothing down his still-ruined shirt and now-wrinkled trousers. He picked at a wet spot on said shirt while grimacing again.

"It's only come. You should taste it. I wish you would've. It tastes wonderful!"

He stared down at me, a wrinkle appearing between his eyebrows as he frowned. "What's wrong with you today?"

"Wrong?" Nothing was wrong, nothing at all! "Life's *wonderful*!"

His frown deepened. "Chad…"

"Why can't I be your boyfriend?" I interrupted him. I didn't want to hear whatever he had to say. He didn't seem like it was anything happy.

"You're my student—and I love my boyfriend."

"Not enough." I wrapped my hand around my cock, which was still hard. If he wasn't going to finish this, I had to. "We're close aren't we? Have been since term started. I mean, I never thought I'd have such a young, fit teacher, you know? And you almost always kept me back when the rest of the class finished."

"Because I'm worried—"

"You want me. You just proved it in the biggest way."

"I can get fired for this!" He backed away from me, but he couldn't seem to rip his eyes away from my cock.

Gotcha!

I stroked it faster to give him a proper look at what he was missing out on.

Maybe if I gave him enough of an incentive, he'd kneel besides me and swallow me down, sucking me to completion.

Maybe he'd even let me come in his mouth.

Maybe he'd swallow.

That would be so hot.

"You can do anything you want to me." I was panting by now, chasing my second orgasm. "I'm at your mercy. You can fuck me into the floor. You can tie me up. Manhandle me!" I sat up, hand still busy wanking myself off.

His eyes were wide and staring at me, but not exclusively at my dick anymore. His gaze was darting from my cock to my face and back again.

Repeat, repeat, repeat.

I came with a loud shout and I swear stars tinkled before my eyes as I collapsed in a blissed out heap.

Come to it, they were still there when I opened my eyes again.

When exactly did I close them?

The ceiling in the teacher's lounge had stars painted on them. Flashing stars burning brightly.

Colourful and illuminating.

They were beautiful.

"Chad?" The voice was far off.

Who did it belong to anyway?

Whoever it was, they should be watching the stars too. It wasn't often you saw stars inside.

It was a special occasion.

I wish I owned a camera—this deserved to be taken pictures of.

"I love you."

I was on my feet and had jumped on Dion before I could even process what was happening. "I love you too!"

I hugged him tight, but he didn't seem to hold onto me as tightly.

Hadn't he just said he loved me? He should hold me, he shouldn't ever want to let me go! I was his and he was mine—

"We belong together!"

"No!" Dion managed to extricate himself from me. Why would he even want to really? His expression was full of love and caring. His brown eyes were so warm. "Chad!"

I spun around in a twirl, almost managing to tumble over the fallen chair, but instead I kept my balance and I even put it up properly.

I sat down in it and spun it around. "Together we can conquer the world!"

"I'm calling 999."

"Who's sick?" I swivelled around to face him. He had his mobile phone out and was pressing buttons.

"You are!" He glanced up, expression seemingly scared and angry—but then it morphed into the loving one I'd just seen.

God, he loves me.

"I'm happy!" I threw my arms up, wriggling my

fingers up towards the stars. I could almost reach them—just a little bit—

"I love you, Chad."

"I told you I love you too!" I swivelled around on the chair again, around and around and around. "I've loved you since the day I met you, the day I walked into the classroom and saw you standing there. So tall and handsome and posh. And you gave me the time of day, like, when no one else ever has. You fell for me too then, didn't you? I *knew* it!"

I was out of the chair and over by the door.

My body thrummed with energy and I needed to do something about it.

"Chad, get dressed."

Back around, pick up my boxers and jeans, pull them on, and then I was ready to *really* conquer the world.

How could I not?

I was invincible!

No one could resist me.

Dion murmured something and when I turned, I saw he was on the phone. "Who are you calling?"

"Bloody 999." He frowned at me now. Where was the gaze full of love from earlier?

"You don't have to do that, I'm not sick. I'm perfectly healthy. Look, I'm even hard again!" I held my arms out and bent my head to look down at my crotch. My erection pressed against the front of the zipper. "You need the A&E, since you can't seem to get it up again. Now *that's* not normal." I spun around to the door again. "I have to go. Things to do, people to bang, a life to live!" I skipped ahead. "You stay here and watch the stars. They're beautiful!"

"What stars?" He asked, incredulous, but then I was out the door and he was out of my mind.

He couldn't give me what I needed.

So I needed to go find someone who could.

And I knew just the right person for it.

CHAPTER 2

*T*he door slammed open without warning and I stumbled inside.

I would've fallen flat on my face if Wynn's broad chest hadn't been there to steady me.

"The fuck are you doing?"

I straightened myself and looked up at Wynn.

He glared down at me.

I guess I'd been leaning on said door, knocking a bit too incessantly.

But no mind.

My gaze took him in, from the ruffled, shaggy black hair all the way down his tall, gangly form to his black socks. He wore a tight vest and jeans, all black.

He looked *good*.

"Fuck me." I crowded into him again, regretting straightening up in the first place. If I'd just stayed against him I could've done my work without having to use my words.

"No." Wynn pushed me away, but he did slam the door shut behind me too, so obviously he was just playing hard to get.

"What'd you mean no? You're always up for a shag." I jumped his back, my arms going round his neck and my legs around his hips. "I need it." I rutted against him, letting him feel just how in need I was. "Come on. Come *on*. Fuck me. You've never minded before. Madison can join too. You can double fuck me. Come on, Wynn. I *need* it. I *want* it. It's not enough."

He stood stock still. "What's not enough?"

"The shag I just had. I shagged him, you know, *finally*. And it was amazing—but I need more. He didn't want to give me more, but you will. You always do. I can always count on you. He told me he loved me and he fucked me, and we're great, but now I need you. Need you so much." I raked my nails over his chest, the way I knew he liked.

He breathed deeper, then strode off to his bedroom, me still clinging to his back, where he proceeded to dump me on his big, soft bed.

I'd spent more nights than I could count on that bed, both sleeping and fucking.

"Who'd you shag?" He loomed over me, arms crossed over his chest. He looked positively magnificent.

I shimmied out of my jeans and boxers for the second time that day, throwing them haphazardly away without so much as looking at them. My cock was hard again, ready to go for the third orgasm.

Is it the third?

I wasn't sure.

"Dion fucked me." And then I'd got off once on my own. Had I got off earlier today? I couldn't recall. Anyway, I was going for the record. "Come on, come on, come *on*," I urged, spreading my legs wide open.

Wynn's gaze dropped from my face to my package.

My straining, leaking, ready-to-go package.

I knew he was affected.

I could see his own dick pressing against his jeans.

Wynn was a selfish bastard—if he wanted sex and it was offered, he'd take it. I used it to my advantage now.

I was unceremoniously flipped over and I grinned as my face was smashed into one of Wynn's many pillows.

Yes, yes, yes.

He wasted no time, only snapped a condom on then rammed into me.

My whole body jerked forward by the sudden rough motion, and I gripped onto the headboard to avoid hitting my head against it.

Wynn might be tall and lanky, but he was *strong*, and he lifted the lower half of my body up like I weighted nothing. He took me forcefully, the way he preferred sex.

I liked it too, the way he took complete control and had his way with me.

I wasn't the one in control now. I didn't have to do anything, just lay there and let him fuck my body into exhaustion.

Afterwards, it took a while for me to move.

Wynn sat beside me, cross-legged and dressed proper again. He was studying his nails when I finally managed to turn my head to look at him.

"What are you on?" He didn't turn to me, but I was pretty sure I was the only one there, so it had to be me he was talking to.

I stretched out, enjoying the soreness in my body.

"You're tripping, Chad, so *what* are you *on*?"

"Nothing." On? I hadn't taken any drugs today. "I only took some yesterday—and only what *you* gave me."

I rolled over onto my back and twinkling lights caught my attention.

A smile spread slowly on my lips, almost splitting my face. "You've got stars too. So beautiful." I stretched my hand up again, like I'd done in the teacher's lounge.

They seemed to twirl around it, but I couldn't feel anything.

Both my arms were suddenly at either side of my head in a tight grip, and Wynn straddled my chest as he glared down at me. "You're hallucinating. What're you on? Amphetamines, cocaine, *heroin*?"

"Nothing!" My blessed out feelings from sex disappeared in a puff of smoke. Left was only anger and I bucked against him, fighting his grip on me. I had nothing on him though, so I was stuck there until he saw fit to release me. That only made my anger flame up. "I'm on nothing, you fucker! Let. Me. GO!"

"Fuck if I will!" His grip tightened painfully.

"Chad."

My head whipped around. "Whose there?"

"No one's here!" Wynn didn't even bother to check.

"You've got someone over?" There'd been a voice. I'd *heard* it.

"I love you, Chad."

"You love me?" I whipped my head back to face him. He was so close to me our noses almost collided.

He jerked back, his grip slacking a bit. "What?"

"You told me. Just now."

He cocked his head to one side, seemingly more calculating now than angry.

"Chad. Chad. I love you. Chad."

"You got a gal over?" It was a female voice, definitely a female voice.

It was familiar too.

But I didn't really know any women, except my aunt.

And why would my aunt be at Wynn's flat? She didn't like Wynn, she would rather see me friendless than with him.

"You're losing it." Wynn scrambled off me.

It took me a few second to realise I was free—but when I did I was out of the bed and over the floor. The voice was speaking to me again, but I couldn't see anyone.

Wynn had a small balcony on his flat and the door was slightly ajar.

I wrenched it open and almost fell out onto the small, limited space.

"Mum?" I remembered that voice. It was *hers*. It came from ahead of me, but I still couldn't *see* her.

I climbed the railing. "Mum!" It was cold and windy, and only then did I realise I was naked except my shirt, but my mum was speaking to me. She wanted me here, she wanted me to—

"Chad, no!" Someone grabbed me around the waist and then I was falling—until my back hit the ground so hard I had the breath knocked out of me.

I blinked my eyes open to see Wynn bending over me, face in a grimace.

"Why did you stop me?" I raged, pushing at him. "You can't stop me! She wanted me to fly! I can fly like a bird!"

"More like smash your body to pieces on the tarmac," he said drily.

He easily fended away my hands, rolled me over, and pinned them on my back. The cold floor of the balcony seemed to sear against my skin. What if my skin actually stuck to it? What if my limp dick did? What if when I stood up, part of my flesh would be ripped off and left there?

It was as if a light had been switched off.

The good feelings from earlier were gone.

The vivid colours were nowhere to be seen, neither were the stars.

I couldn't hear mum's voice anymore.

She'd *left* me.

I was all on my own again.

I had *no one.*

"Come on. Get inside." Wynn wrenched me up on my feet, but it was only because he half lifted, half dragged me, I even managed to get inside at all.

He dropped me on his bed and I curled into a ball, staring bleakly at the opposite wall.

A brief flick of my eyes revealed a dull ceiling, devoid of stars.

I wished they'd come back.

"You're not leaving here until the drugs are out of your system."

It wasn't like I could get off the bed even if I'd wanted to, so that was perfectly okay with me.

TWO DAYS later I finally trudged home.

That was two days of lying apathetic in Wynn's bed, with him prodding me and Madison gazing at me with his constantly wide eyes.

"What's wrong with him?" I'd heard Madison asked Wynn the first day when he came over.

"Fuck if I know." Wynn wasn't exactly the most nurturing type, though I never doubted he cared about me. If he hadn't, he never would've allowed me to stay in his *bed.*

I'd watch him physically throw people he was displeased with out of his flat several times, at parties he'd held.

I was one of the lucky ones—who had Wynn as a friend. The only sliver of luck I'd ever had. Madison was even more so, as he was Wynn's boyfriend.

Though they had a strange relationship. Worked out for me though as I could always crash at Wynn's place, and be in his bed, without Madison being worried or jealous about it.

Though, come to that, I wasn't sure if he knew Wynn and I had sex regularly. He'd never been around the times Wynn and I had hit the sack.

Did Wynn tell him everything, since Madison was his boyfriend and all?

It was hard to tell if Madison liked me or not though, since he was always so strange.

Speaking of sex… I'd had sex with Dion.

At least I thought I had.

Had I hallucinated that too or had it been real?

Jumping my teacher in the teacher's lounge surely wouldn't be something I'd hallucinate, but at the same time it also was one of the stupidest things I'd ever done. Not the sex, obviously, because I'd had my eye on him since the beginning of the year, but having sex in school.

I didn't want to get him fired.

But it had been good.

If it had happened at all.

I scared myself.

I knew I was unpredictable, that my mood could switch to the opposite in seconds. But when I hallucinated… that scared me more than anything else did. More than my dad when he was in a real vile mood.

I must be going mad.

Who hallucinated stars and heard voices of their dead mother?

But I was also so happy when in those moods, and sex was so much better then as well. Everything felt good.

Until I did something extremely stupid that could kill me, like climbing on top of the railing of Wynn's third floor flat, naked, in the middle of January.

It was a wonder I hadn't lost my footing and fallen to the ground below me instead of back on Wynn's balcony—or that I hadn't got pneumonia out of it all.

Was it the drugs?

I was so sure I hadn't taken any that day, but maybe the drugs from the day before had stayed in my system?

Or… had I taken drugs?

My memory was fuzzy, I couldn't remember with certainty.

If it was the drugs... then my hallucinations and extreme mood had an explanation. If I hadn't then I must be going completely mad. No sane person had hallucinations like the one's I'd had.

Like the ones I *had*.

They hadn't just happened two days ago. It was the same every time. Brighter colours, stars sometimes or some other shapes, and voices.

And the sex... I wanted sex as much as the next bloke, but when in those moods I tended to be insatiable.

Something must be seriously wrong with me and it scared me to death. Maybe one day I'd just jump out of a window or a balcony, like I'd tried, and end it all. Wouldn't that be neat? No more messed up me.

My house came into sight and I sighed in relief. Even after staying in bed for two whole days—days I'd completely missed college—all I was looking forward to was to bury myself in my own bed.

But once I entered the hallway and heard loud, slurring voices from the living room I knew I wouldn't be getting peace enough to sleep.

Dad was drunk, his usual state of being, and he had his drunkard mates over as well.

Brilliant.

As if my day wasn't bad enough.

"You!" Dad had caught sight of me trying to tip-toe past the door.

I debated just heading up to my room, but with my luck lately he'd just follow me and break my door down.

Best to deal with him downstairs where I could at least run out the door if he—if they—got too rowdy.

So I shuffled into the living room with my head bowed. Better not provoke him. He never toned down his viciousness towards me, even with his mates there. Sometimes, them being there to watch made him even worse. Depended on his mood, really, which hard to gauge with just one word spoken.

"Bring me a beer." Dad threw his empty bottle away. It rolled over the floor only to stop once it hit the wall. I followed its journey with my eyes before slumping into the kitchen. Our fridge hardly ever contained anything edible—it was filled up with bottles and six-packs of beer.

I slunk back in and handed him the bottle, not going closer to him than I absolutely had to, hoping he was only too lazy to get up so I could get away unscathed.

"So your teacher rang me the other day."

My blood ran cold. So much for getting away unscathed. "I didn't do anything."

"You must've, else he wouldn't be ringin', would he?" Dad leered at me.

I took a step back. The route was clear to the hallway.

Only problem was my feet were suddenly swiped out from underneath me and I fell with a loud bang to the floor.

Dad laughed along with his group of drunken mates.

I wondered if the arseholes would be laughing if it had been their own sons falling face first to the floor.

My nose felt tender, and my cheekbone hurt, but I didn't dare touch either. It would only encourage him more. My shoulder flashed with pain as I pushed myself up in a sitting position.

"How old are you now?" Dad bent over in his chair so he could glare down at me.

"Nineteen," I muttered.

"Old enough to take care of yourself then, aren't you?"

Oh God.

No no no.

Dad, don't.

"I haven't got anywhere else to go."

"Find someplace."

"How am I supposed to do that? I'm in college. I haven't got money for a place of my own." I got on my feet and stumbled back. He couldn't do this to me. He couldn't throw me out.

"And I haven't got money to keep you fed."

Like I'd ever been properly fed since Mum died. "Dad, please…"

"You hear him beg?" Dad looked around at the assortment of blokes gathered. They all laughed again. I took another step back, away from them. "You wanna beg properly, you get on your knees."

They all leered at me now. "What? Dad—"

"On your fucking knees!" Dad bellowed, his face turning red with rage.

I wasn't getting on my knees in front of middle-aged men leering at me. I swore the one sitting closest to Dad, but further back so Dad couldn't see him unless he turned, kneaded his crotch.

God, no!

I turned tail and fled.

The door slammed against the railing outside when I pushed it open, while I tripped on my own feet over the threshold and tumbled down the stairs. I groaned as the gravel dug into my skin, but I had to get away.

I couldn't let those old perverts get to me.

"Chad!" A hand was on my shoulder, startling me into pushing away forcefully. Had someone followed me out anyway?

But when no hands touched me again, I turned my head. And it wasn't any of Dad's drunken mates —it was Dion.

CHAPTER 3

"*W*hat're you doing here?"

My gaze darted towards the door, which was still open. Loud voices could be heard from inside. It was obvious said voices belonged to drunk men what with all the slurring, cursing and sounds of bottles clicking together.

"You haven't been in school in two days." Dion frowned worriedly down at me. He still had his palms out in the general sign for peace. "And today's Friday."

"What's that got to do with anything?" I got back up on my feet. It was more difficult this time around, as my meeting with the gravelled path was more damaging than my meeting with the carpeted floor inside.

"I didn't want to worry about you all weekend." He took a step closer, presumably since he saw me struggling, but he didn't touch me again. He seemed torn.

"Nothing to worry about." Even though there *was*.

"What was that on Wednesday?" He cocked his head slightly, taking me in from top to bottom.

I felt like I was on display—and the sound of the drunken voices from inside made my skin crawl.

"Walk with me?" I had to get away. I couldn't stay here right now. I'd go back in the night, or in a couple of days, maybe Dad's mood would've passed by then. Maybe he'd even forgotten what he'd said.

Dion fell into step besides me. He had his hands buried in his thick jacket's pockets.

My own thin one wasn't much for keeping the cold out, but I was used to it.

Still, his seemed rather warm and snuggly.

"So?" He prodded eventually when I failed to say anything.

"So what?"

"So what was that on Wednesday?"

"Sex?" I hedged, though I knew that part wasn't what he meant.

"That's another thing I want to talk to you about."

My stomach fell. "What about it?"

"It can't happen again." Of course it couldn't. "I mean, it was good and all, but I have a boyfriend, and I want to stay with him."

"So you don't like me?" It slipped out before I could filter it. I should've told him it was no big deal, that it was just sex. That was the best thing to do when you were dumped—but with him I couldn't put up that tough facade.

Maybe that was because I truly did like him.

Because I was a little bit in love with him, even.

"I do, Chad. Don't think I don't. But Jeremy and I… We've been together two years. I want to be with him and I can't have anything jeopardise that. Not anything *else*." He already had once. With me.

"You can have me on the side." I'd take the crumbs if need be. All I wanted was him. I'd never wanted anything for myself before now.

"I'm not a cheater." His hand emerged from his pockets to rub over his eyes. He wasn't wearing the glasses he normally wore at college, I took a sudden notice of. He looked just as hot, less teacherly, with his glasses off.

"Except you are," I pointed out, perhaps a bit cruelly, but it was the truth.

He'd had sex with me.

He'd been willing, at least as far as I knew.

I couldn't trust my mind half the time.

All the time, really.

I couldn't trust that this was real, that I wasn't still hallucinating it. But then again, if I'd been hallucinating, he certainly wouldn't be telling me we couldn't hook up again.

And I would feel a lot better about myself.

He tipped his head back, gazing skywards. "It's not who I am, Chad. I know I did cheat on him with you, but it's not *who* I am. I'm not a person who cheats on his partner."

He was so adamant about it there must be something personal in it. "Someone ever cheat on you?" I scuffed the dirty toe of my Converse against the pavement.

"Not on me, no." His tone was final.

I took the hint.

No talking about it.

"Where are you heading?"

I shrugged. "Don't know."

I'd already imposed on Wynn for two days.

I could stop by my aunt's café perhaps. If anything, I'd get something good and proper to eat.

"Down to Soho."

He gave me a shrewd glance. "Clubbing?"

"No." It wasn't a wrong assumption of his though. I did it often enough. "I'm stopping by my aunt's café. Getting something to eat. You can come with if you want?"

"I shouldn't," he muttered, again dragging his hands over his face.

"That's okay." I hung my head, disappointment weighing me down.

He was silent for a long moment, and then he shuffled closer and bumped his shoulder with mine. "Tell you what, I'll buy you a meal and then we can talk."

He still wanted to talk? I thought we'd covered the basics—that sex wouldn't be on the table again.

But I wasn't about to say no to spend some time with him outside of college, so I didn't say anything.

If I opened my mouth I was afraid I'd ruin the opportunity.

"You seem good today."

I startled. "What?"

"Like your normal self, I mean. Wednesday was—hell, Chad, I don't know what that was."

"Drugs," I croaked out, because that was a better explanation than the alternative.

That I should be locked up in a mental facility.

His head turned towards me so fast I was afraid he'd get a crick in his neck. "You do drugs?"

"Sometimes." What'd he think was wrong with

me if not drugs? Did he just think I was a complete mental case?

In that case he'd be right.

"I wish you wouldn't do that."

"It's my life," I muttered, stung by the worry in his tone. He didn't want to keep having sex with me, but he was going to treat me food and he obviously cared.

Why did he have to be taken?

Why'd he have to have a bloody boyfriend he didn't want to cheat on?

I wouldn't have minded being the mistress, so to speak. As long as I had some part of him.

"It's dangerous, Chad. Besides, don't you think you should focus on your A-levels? You chose to take them—and you don't want to fail the year again, do you?"

And he had to remind me just how much of a failure I really was. "I'm not smart enough."

"Sure you are. You just need some help with the reading and writing—"

"Not the dyslexia thing again," I groaned.

I'd heard it before.

I was just stupid.

There was no need on putting a learning disability on it. Coupled with the rest of my shaky sanity, I wasn't fit for anything.

"I really think we should look into it—"

"No." I cut him off shortly. "I try my best, but it's not good enough. There's nothing else I can do."

I'd accepted the fact I wasn't going to get anywhere academically.

Why did I even bother going back to college, really?

It was those good days, when I thought I could do anything in the world and be best at it.

Too bad reality always came back to shove it up my arse I wasn't good for anything.

"You can get help. The college will adjust to your needs."

Why couldn't he just drop the bloody subject?

"I don't want to talk about it." Getting help… as if.

Could they help me make sense of the words I wrote?

Could they help my handwriting and my grammar?

I thought not.

Better to just accept things the way they were. Less sorrow and heartbreak and crushing disappointment that way.

He finally dropped it and we walked in awkward silence downtown.

It wasn't that far, only about twenty more minutes until we reached our destination.

Harriet's Café the sign read, and it led into a small and homey café. It was never crowded, but it seemed to be doing good. At least Harriet had never complained about it *not* going good.

My aunt wasn't to be seen, which was just as good as I was there with Dion now. I didn't want her asking questions—that would be uncomfortable both for her and him.

I'd seen Harriet's employees before, but I hadn't a clue what their names were. Today the black-haired bloke who always looked so serious was behind the counter.

Dion gave his order in a strong, confident voice while I mumbled mine out. I didn't really care what I ate, as long as it was something that would fill me up.

"How often do you do drugs?" Dion asked once we'd sat down at the most reclusive table in the corner.

I glanced up at him, but upon finding his gaze on me, I quickly bowed my head again. "Don't know. Now and then."

He folded his arms on the table. I guess he was getting ready for a confrontation. "You an addict?"

"No." I shook my head to emphasise it. "I'm not addicted. I don't crave drugs."

"Then why take them?"

"Sometimes they make things better. They make *me* feel better."

I knew he was regarding me by the way the hairs stood on end in my neck. "Are things real bad at home?"

I drew in a breath and held it.

How was I supposed to answer that?

I'd been asked more times than I could count at school ever since my mum died and I'd always denied it. Even when the child services did investigate, Dad managed to actually stay sober and fool them we had a proper healthy relationship.

And I only had my dad, so I wasn't about to rat him out. If I didn't have him, I wouldn't have anywhere to live.

I knew, rationally, that Harriet wouldn't let me live on the streets, that she'd gladly take me in, but I couldn't expose her to me and my volatile mood. I was afraid I'd hurt her.

When it came to Dad I didn't care—besides, it wasn't like I *could* hurt him—and with Wynn he was always in control, even when I wasn't in control of myself. He kept me grounded even if he had to hold me down to do it.

But Harriet… she had no idea what a mental case I was and I didn't want her to know. She was kind and sweet, and she reminded me so much of Mum it physically hurt sometimes. She deserved better than a messed up nephew barging into her personal space.

"Chad?" Dion's finger prodded my arm, snapping me out of my thoughts.

"Hm?"

"Are things real bad at home?"

Right, that had been his original question and my thoughts had taken it in hand and run away with it.

"Not really." I was lying through my teeth. I was pretty sure he could tell too.

What happened if I did confess? I was of age. It wasn't like the child services could enter the picture again. I was on my own now.

Being on my own really wasn't such a good idea.

"Did you tell your boyfriend? About us, I mean, about Wednesday." I fiddled with my fingers to avoid having to look at him.

He cleared his throat. "I did, yeah."

"You're still together?"

"Yeah." The relief was loud and clear.

It crushed me—the tiniest bit.

Okay, it crushed me *a lot*.

Why couldn't he care about me the way he cared about his boyfriend? The answer was obvious, at least to me. He should be *lucky* he didn't care about me that way.

I only brought bad luck and heartbreak.

"Chad…" He reached across to take my hands in his. His were a lot bigger than mine; they engulfed them. "You deserve better than this. Someone who loves only you. Someone who isn't a decade older than you and your teacher, besides."

"What do you know about what I deserve?" It came out petulant, even I heard it, but I couldn't help myself. I *was* petulant.

How could he come here and say I deserved better than him?

I didn't.

I didn't even deserve him, for all I wanted him.

Our food arrived and he pulled his hands back. I felt the loss of them just as deeply as the knowledge that he'd never want me enough. I'd lost my appetite. The food was good, I knew that from experience, but looking at it now made my stomach turn.

"I can't." I pushed my plate away so forcefully it slammed into his plate, nearly toppling both into his lap.

He scrambled to catch them, and by the time he could move his focus back to me, I was already out the door.

CHAPTER 4

I wasn't clear on how exactly I got there, I must've walked away from the café in a daze, but now I was crying on Wynn's shoulder.

Wynn, on the other hand, sat stock still besides me, gaze trained ahead. As I'd mentioned before, he wasn't the nurturing type and having me crying all over him wasn't part of his comfort zone.

Still, that he even allowed it to happen spoke volumes of just how much he cared about me.

"You're the only one who cares." Sobs made it difficult to get the words out, but I managed. I hoped he understood me. "No one cares about me, Wynn. I really liked him and he fucked me over. He's with his boyfriend. And he's staying with him. What we had meant nothing."

Wynn awkwardly patted my upper arm. "Did you really have anything in the first place? Besides that shag three days ago, anyway."

"You know we've been talking since the start of term. He's always holding me back, asking me if I'm okay. Giving me extensions if I need it. We *talked* and I thought... I thought he'd come to care about me as much as I care about him."

I drew my legs up and crowded even further into Wynn's personal space, which definitely had to both annoy him and make him uncomfortable, but he still sat there stock still. He let me get it out.

"At least you weren't high this time when you met him."

"I wasn't last time either."

"Of course you were." His patience had limits. He'd reached it. "You were fucking high, Chad. You can't lie to me. I know when people are on drugs. I provide them, remember?"

How could I forget?

How many times had he given me something to trip on? Something to make me feel better?

It worked too, mostly.

Sometimes even too much.

Like last time, my mood seemed to have risen above the elevation of the drugs and taken on a mind of its own. Maybe doing drugs wasn't such a bad idea, considering, since those bouts of very, very good moods weren't something I wanted to give up either.

I didn't want to be miserable all the time.

"Doesn't matter anyway." I sniffled. "He doesn't want me."

"Then he's a right sod." At least someone had a high opinion of me. Higher than I had of myself, even.

The front door opened and shut, and I desperately wiped at my eyes once I realised it meant someone was actually in the flat.

I didn't want anyone to see me cry, besides Wynn, anyway.

Madison's skinny legs came shuffling into view, and his continuously wide eyes stared at me.

"What's wrong with you?" Madison usually sounded flat, like he didn't have much emotion or care about anything, but for once I had to give it to him; he did sound concerned.

Did I look so bad even *Madison* had to dredge forward his emotions?

"His teacher fucked him over. Literally."

I cast Wynn a wounded look while still wiping furiously at my eyes. The tears just wouldn't *stop*. "Thanks a lot, mate. Really."

"No problem." Wynn jerked his head in a short motion that could've been either a nod or a shake.

I took it to be a nod, so it would fit with his words.

Or maybe it was just him being annoyed.

It was hard to tell sometimes.

"I brought dinner." Madison held a plastic bag up. Delicious smells of takeaway came from it and my stomach growled loudly. It wasn't like I'd eaten much of my food at the café.

"I'll get plates and cutlery." Wynn got up from the sofa, and Madison sunk down in his abandoned place.

His eyes darted back and forth between me and the table.

"What?" I asked, since he clearly had something on his mind.

"Your teacher?"

"Yeah." Hadn't Wynn told his boyfriend about my silly crush?

I'd only had it for months, and he'd known about it from the start. He'd had Dion as his teacher too, though Wynn hadn't failed and had to re-do two bloody years of his education, so he'd finished his A-levels two years ago, as one were supposed to do.

"Is he old?"

Why the hell did he want to know how old Dion was?

"Not really. He's the youngest teacher I've ever had. Only ten years older than me."

"That's not so much." Madison's wide eyed gaze was far-away now. I wondered, if he didn't think a decade was much, how old his old boyfriends had been. "You like him?"

"Yeah. He's a real nice guy." Bit cliché though, wasn't it? To fancy my young, hot teacher. I was like the stereotypical character in a teen drama, with the exception of the gay part.

And the mad part.

Wynn came back with plates and cutlery for us, as promised, and disappeared again for a few second to fetch glasses and a bottle of Cola.

Madison had bought a lot of food, so there was no problem dividing it on the three of us.

"Can I crash here tonight again? Dad kind of threw me out."

Wynn only chewed his food, expression bored, but Madison turned to me.

"I'm often thrown out of home too," he said, voice devoid of any particular emotion. It was like he was just stating a fact.

"Really?"

I wonder why.

Whereas I was pretty sure I was going mad and should really be locked up somewhere, Madison was most definitely a mental case.

He was done with his A-levels too—at college was where he'd met Wynn—and it was a wonder no one'd ever taken any action. Maybe he was as good a liar as I was? And his mum was as big a phoney as Dad.

In that case, they'd make a pretty good pair.

What a messed up life we all had.

I wasn't even going to get started on Wynn's. His was just as bad, though of course, I didn't know Madison's exact circumstances, but his off-hand comment suggested they weren't so great.

Certainly something must be wrong for him to turn out the way he was.

While Wynn had been my best mate since lower secondary school, I'd only met Madison through Wynn. While I'd failed my GCSEs and had to take the year anew, Wynn had started his A-levels. When he'd finished his, I'd failed my first year, which I was now retaking. I didn't know why I even bothered, considering how stupid I was.

I hadn't wanted to be like Dad.

That was the sole reason I'd decided to take them in the first place.

I didn't want to end up a mean drunk who never

left his house. I'd end up a mental case instead, locked up in a hospital somewhere in a straightjacket.

It sure wouldn't surprise me if it were to happen.

And soon too.

ON MONDAY, my mood had made a complete switch again.

But I wasn't happy now, nor was I depressed—I was angry.

No, scratch that, I was *fuming*.

My foot tapped the floor through the entire class and my eyes didn't leave Dion.

He, on the other hand, didn't so much as look at me once.

I was absolutely raging and I was ready to pounce the minute class was over, which happened way too slowly for my liking.

Once it was over, the rest of the class spent too bloody long getting their lazy arses out of there.

Once the last person was out and the door shut with a click after his back, I strode up to the front. "How dare you!" I pointed my finger at Dion, accusingly.

He startled at my voice. Clearly he'd thought I'd already left.

My eyes narrowed. "You think you're getting off that easy? You're a bloody prick, s'what you are. Shagging me first then you won't have me once you've tasted the goods. I'm not good enough for you?"

"Wha—Chad—"

"Don't you dare say my name!" I quivered, that's how angry I was. "You used me. Then you cast me aside. Tell you what, you can fuck right off! I don't need you. I can do a hell of a lot better, just like you said."

I backed off from him, going backwards towards the door.

"What if I tell, huh? What'll you do then? You'll be in so much trouble for shagging your own student. Doesn't matter if I'm of age or not."

Now he looked stricken.

Good. Let him feel it.

"Chad, please. I'm begging you. Not just because I'd very much like to keep my job, which I *do*, but because I didn't mean to use you. I wanted to help you."

"Good job of it you did." My tone was snarling, condescending. I hated him for doing this to me, for making me feel like I did. For acting like he cared and then doing a double turn and tossing me aside.

"Chad…" He stepped towards me hesitantly.

"Don't!" I couldn't stand to have him near me.

If he came within touching distance, I would deck him. I really would, even if I wasn't so sure I'd do any damage.

Still, the message would be the same.

"You on drugs again?" He was wary, I could tell, but he stayed where he was.

"Why does everyone presume it's drugs?" I spat, my hackles rising even more by his assumption. I wasn't on any bloody drugs!

"Because the mood you're in right now… It's not you. It's not who you are."

"Then I guess it is drugs, then." It was who I was. It was who I was when I'd been used.

I wasn't a pushover.

He couldn't just barge around however he pleased. I wasn't some kind of doormat for him to stomp upon. I was a person and I had feelings, and I had rights, and he was a tosser for just casting me aside like I meant *nothing*.

"Did you ever really care about me? Because really, I don't think you ever did. You just wanted your cake and eat it to and once you've had a taste you threw the rest aside without thought to how it'd feel for *me*. I think I kinda loved you, you know, but I don't anymore. I hate you. You have no idea just how much I hate you. I don't ever want to see you again."

I couldn't look at him anymore, at his face, how he battled between different emotions.

So I left the classroom.

I stopped by the administration on my way out, delivered a rather forceful "I fucking quit this lousy school!" and slammed my student ID down in front of the startled woman.

Then I was out of there.

Free, for the first time in my life.

No more school for me, no more feeling stupid by not being able to read or write or understand all the bullshit. I could do whatever I wanted now. I could find a job, maybe move out of my dad's house if the pay was okay.

And I certainly wouldn't be seeing Dion again.

I'd had enough.

Good riddance.

Good riddance to the college, to Dion, to fucking up every single thing. I could do loads better without it.

My mood definitely switched from enraged to hopefully optimistic as I stalked through the streets. Now all I had to do was find a job that paid reasonably well—and then I'd be fine.

CHAPTER 5

3 WEEKS LATER

*T*urned out being out of school wasn't much better than being in it.

Though at least I earned some money now, even if it was crap pay for crap work.

I still hadn't managed to move out of Dad's house either, but at least he hadn't threatened to throw me out on the streets again. I knew he'd get back to it though, if he could manage to wrap his mind about anything, but at the moment it didn't matter.

I was stuck there, if I wanted to be or not.

The house was rank, smelling of spilled beer and vomit. If I hadn't been so hung over myself, I would've left.

As it was, I only wanted my bed. I hoped no one'd been in my room.

"Bloody hell you doin' here?" The slurred voice came from the living room doorway.

I turned slowly. If I moved too quickly, I was afraid I'd black out. Last night was still a blur. "I live here."

"You're old enough to provide for yourself." My dad stumbled closer, a Vodka bottle in one hand. I wasn't surprised to see it was almost empty.

I wasn't surprised he was back to this topic either. I knew it would come up again sometime. Seemed this was that time now.

"Believe me, I'm working on it." It just wasn't easy to find jobs that paid well enough to support myself when I hadn't even been able to finish college.

"Are you talkin' back at me, you little wanker?"

I took a step back, but dad advanced, all the more steady on his feet now.

"I'm not. I swear. I'm not. I'm sorry." I couldn't deal with my dad right now. I couldn't.

Not now, not ever.

When was I ever going to get away from this hell?

"You're sorry?" He slurred a lot, clearly pissed out of his mind. "That's all that ever comes out of your mouth, innit?"

I didn't know what to say, what could placate him, so I stayed quiet. I didn't want to rile him up any further. That never led to anything good for me.

"Answer me, you tosser!"

I flinched.

I hated it when he yelled; it led to bad things. It had ever since Mum died. I couldn't remember what it'd been like before. I had a suspicion my mum had shielded me from him back then, but I couldn't know for sure. I'd only been eleven when she died.

"I don't know what to say, Dad." I kept my head bowed. I'd be better off not provoking him by looking him in the eyes.

It was my mistake.

It was why I didn't see it coming.

Not until the Vodka bottle connected with the side of my head.

I cried out and stumbled back, only to trip over a pair of shoes carelessly tossed aside.

I fell to the floor.

My shoulder took the brunt of it, and it hurt *so* much—but Dad was on me the next moment and the pain in my shoulder was nothing against what I had coming.

It was a relief when I blacked out.

MY EYES FLUTTERED OPEN.

I stared up at the discoloured ceiling for several

long minutes, trying to get my bearings back. I was still in the hallway, still lying on the floor where I'd fallen.

My whole body hurt.

It hurt to *breathe*.

I lifted my arm slowly to check myself over. My stomach was tender and my ribs hurt like a bitch. Dad must've kicked me pretty hard. Or kicked me repeatedly.

It was something he liked to do when I was down.

I was used to it.

I flicked my tongue out to wet my lips and was met with a metallic taste. My lips, one or both, I wasn't sure which, were split and bleeding.

I felt my face with shaking hands and encountered a scrape on my cheek and tender, swollen skin. The scrape must've been from the bottle. It had probably broken when Dad hit me in the head with it. The tender skin, well… either I was covered in bruises, or I was going to *be* covered in bruises.

When I tried to push myself up, but the world tilted around me. My stomach protested loudly and I rolled over onto my side as it emptied itself right there in the hallway.

Dad's going to kill me for this.

He was probably going to kill me anyway, one way or another, just for the hell of it.

I managed to crawl up onto my knees. I bent over as my body ached and my ribs felt like they were in danger of piercing through my skin. Or my lung; whatever it was they were pressed up against in there.

I have to get out of here.

I couldn't hear my dad, but I knew he must be around. He had to be. He never left home unless he needed a refill on his alcohol. Mostly his mates brought it to him, as he himself couldn't be arsed to do anything except drink it.

I carefully pushed myself to my feet. I was glad I hadn't taken my hoodie off, because I was in no shape to get it back on. I thanked whatever sliver of luck I had left for that as I stumbled out the door and down the steps of the house.

My legs gave out after the last step, and I fell with a pained groan to the gravelled driveway.

The gravel dug into the skin of my palms.

I slowly got myself back up on my feet. I pulled my hood up, hoping to hide most of my face from view, as I stumbled towards the street.

It was daylight, but other than that, I had no idea what time it was. I'd had no idea what time it'd been when I'd come home, and I certainly had no idea how long I'd been out of it.

Where am I going to go?

I had no one.

I couldn't go to Harriet. She'd call the police in an instant. I'd never told her what it was like to live with my dad. I didn't want her involved in the mess that was my life.

She was good, she was nice, she was *warm*. She didn't need the poison that was me and my dad ruining her life.

I couldn't go back to Wynn's place either. Not looking like I did.

Wynn could see me pissed or stoned out of my mind, but if he saw me beaten up like this I couldn't know how he would react. What he would do.

He was volatile—and it was impossible to tell what kind of mood he was in at any given time.

Who else have I got?

The answer was simple; I had no one.

No one gave a shit about me, and it was partly my own fault for always pushing people away.

Only Wynn knew me—no one else. He was the only one who knew a sliver of what was really going on, but he couldn't see me like this.

Harriet had tried to set me up with some kind of group therapy. She thought I was still struggling with the trauma of losing my mum. Of course that was a part of it, it couldn't not be, but it wasn't everything. The last part, the really *big* part, was my dad.

Dion...

Thoughts of him invaded my mind.

I'd managed pretty well not to think about him for the last few weeks, but he was always there just out of reach.

He'd always been worried about me, from the very first class of his I'd been in. He'd asked me repeatedly to stay back after classes, always asking me how I was doing. He'd always given me extensions when I hadn't handed my work in on time.

He was kind, he seemed to care. He had—

Dion had sex with me on school property and it had been wonderful. It hadn't been at all like the quick fucks I was used to, the ones I initiated myself, or even the ones I was all but forced into. Nothing could compare to the tenderness he'd shown me. Nothing at all.

Yet he'd chosen his boyfriend over me.

I still couldn't blame him.

I was ashamed for how I'd reacted on my last day at college. I didn't know what had come over me that day, but I wasn't sorry I'd quit college. I'd've failed the exams again anyway.

Maybe Dion would help me out?

He'd said he'd wanted to.

Maybe he still cared just a tiny bit about me and would be willing to act on that. Maybe he'd let me stay for a couple of days until I healed up and could figure out what I was going to do next. He'd always been so kind.

I hoped he still was, even after the way I'd acted three weeks ago.

I knew where he lived.

At least, I knew where he'd lived three weeks ago. I could only pray he still lived there, because if he didn't… then I didn't know what to do.

But then again, what was the chance of him moving away in three weeks? Unless he'd moved before, and not told me. It wasn't like he had to tell me anything, after all.

I sat hunched over on the tube.

I kept one arm wrapped tight around my middle, while the other was braced on my knee. It still hurt to breathe, and I was pretty sure the other passengers were looking at me, but I couldn't find it in myself to care.

I all but dragged myself up to the second-floor flat Dion used to live in and which he hopefully still *did* live in. I'd checked the mailbox on my way up and it still had his name printed on it, so it looked like I was in luck after all.

I leant heavily against the wall next to the door for several moments as I tried to gather my breath. I reached out with the arm that wasn't holding my own waist and knocked two times.

Please let him be home.

Please don't let him send me away.

The door opened slowly and I pushed myself away from the wall.

A man stood there, but it wasn't Dion.

No!

"I— Is Dion here?"

Please, please, please.

My eyes stung and I knew the tears weren't far behind.

"He's not at home right now." The bloke frowned down at me.

I couldn't hold it back anymore. The tears started trickling and the sudden sobs that escaped me hurt ten times more than simple breathing did. "P-please…"

The world spun around me.

I spread both my arms out to try and steady myself against the doorway, but the sudden movement caused my ribs to protest painfully, and I stumbled forward into a pair of strong arms.

CHAPTER 6

I carefully uncurled from the foetal position I'd been in for at least the past few hours.

I'd managed a good couple of hours of blissful sleep before I'd been woken up by Jeremy's voice… and Dion's. After that, my sleep hadn't been so blissful.

I sat up in bed and turned on the lamp placed on the bedside table. My clothes were neatly folded at the end of the bed and I drew them into my lap. They smelled fresh.

He washed them.

My chest constricted and it had nothing at all to do with my bruised ribs. Jeremy had been nothing but kind to me, even knowing who I was.

I'd taken advantage of that, and as a result I was still ruining Dion's relationship. The one he'd broken it off with me to fix in the first place. It wasn't fixed at all, not from what I'd overheard, and that was entirely my fault.

I gingerly changed back into my own clothes.

Then I folded Jeremy's as nicely as possible and put them in the spot where my own had been resting. I smoothed out the covers, making sure it looked as if no one had ever slept in the bed, before I slipped out of the room.

The flat was dark.

Dion and Jeremy had gone to bed hours ago.

I'd waited as long as possible in order to be sure that they actually were asleep.

They'd done enough for me.

I'd leave them be.

I wouldn't wreck anything else between them. I'd done my share.

A picture caught my attention as I made my way through the living room. It was a small, framed portrait standing atop the little corner table between the two sofas.

It was of Dion and Jeremy, smiling into the camera and looking happy.

I lifted the picture up so I could see it better in the dark room.

They looked so comfortable, so at ease.

I want that.

I took a shaky breath.

I want that with someone.

But who would want me? I had *nothing* going for me. Nothing to offer anyone.

It was a bad idea, a *really* bad idea, but I couldn't help it.

I cradled the picture to my chest as I continued through the room and out into the hallway. My old, dirty, beat-up Converse were there, against the wall. I didn't have a jacket, only my thin hoodie. I didn't feel the chill outside when I was drunk or high.

I would tonight, though. It might've been spring, but this early in the morning or late at night—I didn't know what the time was—it would definitely be cold.

The door squeaked when I opened it and I grimaced.

I slipped through when the gap was wide enough and slowly pulled it closed behind me again. It squeaked just as much closing as it had opening. I hoped they weren't light sleepers.

I didn't know what I was supposed to do next. I couldn't go home. I had no idea what mood my dad would be in, and I couldn't face another beating.

The reasons I hadn't gone to Harriet or Wynn in

the first place hadn't changed since last night. I simply had no options. None at all.

I walked slowly through the streets, picture still cradled to my chest and my shoulders hunched against the cold wind. It seemed to blow through me, freezing me from the outside and in, numbing me.

I didn't know how long I walked.

All I knew was I found myself on a bridge—I didn't even know which one—and I stared down at the Thames flowing under me.

What would it be like to jump?

Would the impact kill me or would I drown in the freezing water?

Was it even a far enough fall to do much damage? Or would it be easy to just swim to shore?

One hand braced against the brick of the railing, and I rose up on the toes of my feet. It was just a fall… one fall and then everything would be over. Nothing would have to hurt anymore, no one would be bothered with me, Harriet wouldn't have to *worry*, Dion could fix his relationship without me messing it up for him.

Just one fall…

I braced the other hand on the brick as well, but the sound of the frame thunking against it brought my focus away from the Thames below. I turned the frame over, staring at the two smiling men.

Just like that, the tears overflowed.

I bent down to rest my head against my forearm. I'd known getting involved with my own teacher had been a bad idea, but he'd been so wonderful.

Why'd he have to leave me to go back to his boyfriend?

Why couldn't his boyfriend have been some selfish prick I could hate, instead of the kind man who'd taken care of me?

My tears fell fat and heavy on the glass, obscuring both my vision and the picture itself.

I straightened back up and wiped furiously at the glass with my sleeve. Once all evidence was gone I pressed the back of my hands to my eyes, trying to stem the tears still trickling down my cheeks.

I was a mess, my life was a mess; *everything* was such a mess. What was I supposed to do? I didn't have a single clue and it terrified me.

I'd quit college to get a job, and I'd *had* a job, but I'd been so far away mentally yesterday it had completely skipped my mind that I was supposed to work the midday shift.

When the shift had started, I was likely unconscious on the floor after the beating, and when I'd woken up… I'd run off to Dion's flat and let Dion's *boyfriend* take care of me.

He'd been so kind.

I didn't deserve it.

I didn't deserve anything.

I cradled the picture close and continued along the pavement. I cast one last longing look back at the bridge once I was past it, but I couldn't do it. I couldn't jump.

I walked for a long time.

It was starting to lighten when I finally came to a stop in front of Wynn's building. I looked up at his windows, but they were all dark.

I was frozen through. I wasn't sure I could even unfold my arms from around myself or pry my fingers from the picture I was clutching.

After letting myself into the hallway of the building, I slowly climbed the stairs to Wynn's floor. I contemplated knocking on his door, waking him up and having him let me in, but I couldn't find the strength.

Instead I sunk down the wall next to the door.

My breath stuttered in my chest, which again hurt my bruised ribs. I trembled from the cold. All I managed to do was curl in on myself, resting my forehead against my kneecaps.

I didn't think I'd dosed off, but I must've, because next thing I knew the door at my side opened.

"Fucking hell!"

Wynn's startled yell couldn't even make me raise

my head.

"Chad?"

A pair of big, strong, warm hands were on me, pulling me up.

I swear my joints creaked as I had to uncurl myself. I blinked blearily up at him, and he eventually came into focus. Black clothes, ruffled black hair, and dark eyes.

"The fuck you doing out here?" He shook me and I almost dropped my picture. I clung to it desperately.

Movements stopped—and then his face was in close to mine. "Are you high?"

I shook my head slowly. My brain was still fuzzy —guess I'd been fast asleep after all. I was still freezing too and my teeth chattered.

"Get in." Wynn dragged me into the flat, ignoring the fact that I had my shoes on as he pushed me down on his sofa. He even put a quilt over me, a thick, soft one, which my muddled brain found quite caring. "You sure you're not high?" He stood over me, arms crossed over his chest.

If I hadn't been so cold and exhausted and non-caring, it would've been intimidating.

"I'm not." My voice rasped and I cleared it, which brought about a gasp of pain as my stomach muscles seized.

Wynn was on me the next minute, pushing my hood off my head and dragging my hoodie up to look at my stomach. "Blimey, Chad. That *fucker*."

I had nothing to say. I agreed.

Wynn tucked the quilt over me again. "I'm going to the shop. I've got no food. I'll get you painkillers."

Wynn seemed to be in a good mood, despite being angry about my injuries. "Just the shop?" My voice shook now, I was still freezing cold.

He stared down at me. "Yeah. I'll get some hot chocolate for you too. And tea." He backed off and pointed a finger at me. "You stay there until I get back."

I would have to.

I didn't think I could move on my own.

Everything hurt and my limbs seemed to be frozen into the position I now curled up in. I had no idea how many hours I'd been in the same position, only sitting, outside his door.

I heard the door shut, but it was out of my range of vision from where I was lying. It wasn't like it mattered anyway. Wynn was gone—but at least I lay somewhere comfortable and where I would hope-fully manage to get some warmth back in me.

I pulled the quilt up around my neck, so only my face was bare. It wasn't like anyone was there to see me like this anyway.

Except there was.

I heard shuffling feet long before the person came into my range of vision. I didn't have strength to even so much as turn my head, but now I could clearly see Madison.

He'd stopped in the middle of the living room floor, blinking at me with his big eyes.

I stared back, unable to speak or move.

He blinked some more, probably taking in my bruised and battered face, then he shuffled out of my sight again.

I sighed and let my eyes drop closed.

Madison was *weird*, and that said something, coming from me. He was the oddest person I'd ever had the fortune of meeting—but he was sweet too. I could see what Wynn saw in him when Madison was lucid, though inside he was even more broken than I was. I didn't even know half the stuff he'd been through in his eighteen years.

I nearly fell of the sofa in shock as something warm and moist was pressed to my cheek.

"I'm sorry. I didn't mean to frighten you."

I found Madison's face close to mine when I managed to get my eyes to open again.

He had a wet washcloth in his hand, currently pressed to my face.

"You've got dried blood on you." His teeth bit

down on his lower lip. But that was standard with him. Madison always seemed on edge, nervous, anxious.

"Th-thanks." I concentrated on slowing my breathing, because the faster it was the more I hurt.

His gaze roamed my face. "Who hurt you?"

"My dad." Surely Madison knew that? We were friends, of a sort, and he was with Wynn.

I knew him *through* Wynn, and I couldn't imagine Wynn keeping quiet about my problems to his boyfriend. He might be volatile and a complete tosser at times, but he was a good friend and completely devoted to Madison.

"Oh." He bit down further on his lip.

I started worrying he'd draw blood if he continued like that.

"Yeah. Oh." My eyes fluttered closed again. I was so tired. Everything hurt and I was tired, and all I wanted was to sleep. I didn't feel the hurt when I slept.

Sleep was bliss.

Sleep was like being dead, but without the commitment to actually do it.

Sleep was *good*.

"I know," Madison murmured above me, and my eyes shot open.

Had I been speaking out loud?

His focus was intent on my cheek, where he still tried to wash away the dried blood. He seemed sad though, sad and a bit forlorn. But that was the way he pretty much *always* looked.

"You think death's peaceful?" The question came out before I could stop myself.

"Yeah. Everything's more peaceful than this." The words were spoken with complete seriousness and my stomach clenched.

I knew Madison's life was shit, but he had Wynn, at least. Wynn who loved him and cared about him.

It was more than I had.

I didn't doubt Wynn loved and cared about me too, but that was just as a friend. It wasn't anything more.

He pulled his hand away and leant back against the table. His hands fell to his lap, where the wet washcloth made a stain in his thin shirt. His gaze was to the left of me, seemingly far away. "Are you afraid of dying?"

"Yeah." I thought back to the bridge. It was a fascinating thought, jumping, but I hadn't been able to do it. I didn't know why, it wasn't like I was afraid of heights, but something had stopped me from it.

"I'm not." The fact that he was completely serious scared me.

CHAPTER 7

"Oh for fuck's sake."

I opened my eyes to find Wynn staring down at me. At us, really, as Madison was curled on the other end of the sofa.

"Nothing happened," I said quickly, not wanting him to fly into a rage over some imagined slight towards him. He was quick to anger. And quick to take that anger out on other people. Especially if it involved Madison.

"What?" His eyes narrowed. "Bloody hell you on about?"

"I don't know." I shut my eyes again. Being asleep was so nice, if only I could get back to it.

"I am not taking care of two depressed people. I

draw the fucking line at one. One of you better get your head out of your arse and cheer the fuck up."

I heard him stalk away, into the kitchen.

I opened my eyes again, staring blankly at the dark telly.

The sofa rocked as Madison dragged himself into a sitting position. He sat quietly for a moment, while I continued to stare at nothing, then he poked me lightly in the leg.

I belatedly flicked my gaze over to him. It had taken me several seconds to snap out of whatever I'd been in.

His big eyes blinked at me. "Death."

"What?" Had we still not moved past our previous topic of conversation?

I'd never talked much with Madison—he was always so quiet and strange and just hanging around Wynn—and I'd never had a deep conversation with him like we'd had earlier.

I hadn't known he was so fascinated with death. I wondered if he talked to Wynn about it, if Wynn knew…

"We're alike you and I." He put a hand on my curled up knee. "Maybe we should do it together."

I was officially lost. "Do what together?"

He leaned down, bottom lip trapped in his teeth. "Die."

Discomfort eased its way into me, replacing the hurt of my injuries and the blankness of everything else. "I don't want to die."

"What do you have to live for?"

Nothing.

The answer came momentary.

"Nothing."

He tilted his head. "So…"

"I got your painkillers." Wynn came around the corner and threw the packet of tablets at me. He was more careful with the glass of water, setting in down on the table in front of me.

Water wouldn't do. "Have you got anything stronger?"

He frowned. "Alcohol and tablets don't mix. You know that."

"Since when do you care?" I managed a challenging stare. "You sell drugs, for fuck's sake, and you never cared if any took them with alcohol before. I need a *drink*!"

His face turned stony as he straightened up.

Madison glanced anxiously between us, teeth chewing on his lower lip.

Wynn stalked out of sight then came back and threw a bottle at me.

I yelped.

"Fine! Fuck yourself up. I *don't* care."

I pushed myself up into a sitting position with great difficulty. My battered body protested every single move I made, which only served to higher my desire for a drink. I popped two painkillers, opened the bottle and took a long swig. The tablets went down easily while the alcohol burned.

Wynn stood out on the floor, arms crossed and face neutral. His eyes, however, were a stormy dark. He wasn't happy with me.

But I didn't care. I needed to dull the pain, both the physical one and the mental one, and I needed to forget. Nothing was better to achieve that than getting pissed.

Wynn bent down close to Madison. "Watch him." He pressed a hard kiss to Madison's lips then strode back into the kitchen.

Madison blinked rapidly as he turned to me.

I contemplated him.

He'd just been kissed by his boyfriend… I would've been ecstatic if someone showed such affection to me. But Madison, he didn't seem to feel anything at all. He just looked lost.

"You love Wynn?" Wynn was my best friend. I didn't want him to get hurt. I wasn't sure how long exactly he'd been with Madison, but it must've been at least a year now.

He cocked his head, seeming to contemplate my question. "I don't know what love is."

How could he not know what it was? "I love someone."

Another blink. "Why aren't you with him?"

"He doesn't want me." I reached for the picture on the table and held it out to him. "He has a boyfriend."

Madison ran a long, slender finger over the smiling faces of Dion and Jeremy. "They seem happy."

"They're not. I ruined them." I took another long swallow of the bottle. "That's what I do. I ruin people."

He looked back up at me, eyes curious. It was the first time I'd seen a genuine emotion in them. "Who else have you ruined?"

"My mum. My dad." I shrugged. "I would my aunt too, if I let her get close to me. So I won't let her."

"I ruined my mum." And the curiosity was gone, replaced by emptiness. The only indicator that he felt something was the constant nibbling on his lower lip. "So she keeps telling me."

"At least she's still alive." I wished my mum had been alive. I couldn't know for certain, but I was pretty sure my life would've been a lot different if it was my dad who was rotting in the ground.

His head rolled from side to side. "Mmm, yeah. I haven't got a dad."

I stared at him.

He's so strange.

What exactly did Wynn see in him?

I wouldn't call myself a prime example of healthiness, but there was something seriously *wrong* with Madison. He couldn't be right in the head.

I extracted my picture from his hands and tucked it in my lap.

"All right." Wynn was back, and he promptly sat down in between us. He handed us both steaming mugs. I took mine instantly, not wanting him to drop it on me, as he was perfectly capable of it.

Madison, on the other hand, was more hesitant.

"I added the small marshmallows you like." Wynn pushed it into his hands and Madison's fingers finally wrapped around the mug.

I blew on the hot chocolate as I studied them. Wynn affectionately ruffled Madison's already unruly hair, and Madison's lips stretched in a barely there smile.

"I'm having some people over later."

"For what?" I asked, dubious.

"For socialisation. And drinking."

"Oh." Okay then.

As long as it wasn't some sort of orgy. He'd had one of those once. I'd participated. It had been fun, but my body simply wasn't up for it today. It hurt to *sit*, so anything else would be too much, even with alcohol.

He contemplated me cooly. "You've already got a head start."

"I need it." I held up the hand that held the alcohol and tipped the bottle at him.

"You should mix it with something. You can't drink the alcohol straight from the bottle."

I snorted. "I'm fine."

He gritted his teeth. I could tell he was annoyed. "Know what you're turning into? Your *dad*. That's what he does too."

"Fuck you!" How dared he even say something like that. "What's so wrong with wanting to forget once in a while?"

"Once in a while?" He arched a dark eyebrow. "It was just the other night you were here, pissed. The night before that, pissed. Every night the last two bloody *weeks* you've been pissed."

"There's really nothing wrong in wanting to forget." It was Madison, speaking up in a low voice.

Wynn rounded on him. "You on his side now?

He's ruining himself, fucking himself up. That's not *okay*."

"Says the drug-dealer." I tipped the bottle so some of the liquid poured into my mug. Surely the hot chocolate would taste a whole lot better this way.

It would make me *feel* better, anyway.

Everything to make the pain go away.

Everything to forget, at least for just a little while.

WYNN'S FLAT was packed with people, and it wasn't exactly a big one to begin with. I didn't mind the crowd though, not at all.

"Having fun?"

I turned on wobbly legs to face my best mate.

Wynn smirked at me. It was his standard face, really, when he wasn't being a cold arsehole. It was this condescending smirk that rubbed people the wrong way.

"I nicked a picture today," I confessed. My voice was only slightly slurred. Well, I thought it was anyway. I couldn't hear myself properly.

His black eyebrows rose. "What're you nagging about?"

"A picture." I leaned in closer. "I nicked it. From Dion's flat."

Wynn's eyebrows inched higher. "That bloody teacher broke it off with you. You should forget about him."

"But I have the picture." Such a nice picture it was too, of both Dion and Jeremy.

Jeremy's so kind…

"So where exactly is this infamous picture?" Wynn looked me over and cocked his head.

I looked down at myself, confused, then around the room. "I… I don't know. Where's my picture?" I couldn't lose the picture. It was all I had left.

I *needed* that picture like I needed to breathe.

"Chill out, C. Give me that." Wynn made a grab for my bottle.

"No!" I stepped back and held the bottle out of his reach. "This is my bottle. Don't take it. Find your own."

"Technically it *is* mine." He came closer. "You've had more than enough to drink. Let me take the bottle so you can go find that bloody picture of yours."

"No." I stumbled back and only the firm support of a wall kept me from tumbling to the floor. Wynn gave me a knowing look and held his hand out, demanding, but I petulantly turned away from him as I took a long sip. "You're not my dad."

"If I were, I'd really have to beat the crap out of

you for being such a twat," Wynn commented drily. "I am, however, your mate. So give me that bottle."

"Help me find my picture." I looked around again, but all I could see were *people*. "I need to find my picture."

"What's with you and this picture" He sighed in exasperation. "Seriously, Chad—"

"Wynn!" A bloke pushed through the crown of people and grabbed a tight hold of Wynn's arm. "Wynn! You have to come! It's Madison!"

Wynn's head whipped around. "What?"

I knew I was forgotten then, and I made to walk away, only to be stopped by the unknown guy's next words.

"He's unconscious! We can't wake him up!"

"Where is he?" Wynn started pushing through the throng of people, heading in the same direction the bloke had come from.

I trailed after them, out of curiosity and worry and with a sense of intense foreboding.

Madison was sprawled on the bathroom floor. His eyes were closed and his face pale. His mouth was open slightly and there was vomit there, trickling from his lips onto the white tiles, where there was a bigger puddle.

"Madison!" Wynn fell to his knees next to him. He slapped Madison's face several times, but there was no reaction. "Madison!" Wynn bent to listen to his chest, although I couldn't understand how he could hear anything over the blare of the music and the thumping bass and all the people gathered around us.

I took another long swallow of my bottle. It was almost empty. I looked around again. Had I been in the bathroom earlier? Could I have left the picture here? I needed the picture…

"Madison!" Wynn's was voice was becoming increasingly distressed, frantic. "Someone call 999, dammit! Madison!"

My eyes clouded and I stumbled back. I caught myself against the wall, but I lost the grip I had on the bottle and it fell to the floor.

It broke into pieces and the smell of alcohol seeped out.

I bent over as my stomach seemed to wrench in on itself.

The sick came so fast that I fell to the floor, right in the middle of the alcohol and broken glass, as I choked.

My eyes clouded as I continued to choke.

"Chad!" Wynn called my name now, I heard him, but it was very far away.

I can't breathe…

I can't breathe!

And then not even that mattered because everything got dark.

The last things I noticed were shards of glass pricking my skin and the alcohol seeping into my shirt.

PART II
JEREMY

CHAPTER 8

ONE DAY AGO

*I*t was instinct that caused me to catch the lad as he stumbled forward.

I blinked in surprise as I held his shaking body close, not quite believing just how quickly I'd reacted.

The sight of his face when he'd looked up at me, bruised and bleeding, flashed before my eyes.

"P-please..." He trembled and his tears wetted my tee. "Help me, please!"

I couldn't refuse that plea, even if I'd wanted to. I wasn't heartless. I pulled the lad into the flat and shut the door after us. "What happened to you?" Someone must've done quite a number on him.

He started to shake his head violently, but froze in

mid-shake. He pushed away from me and bent over, both hands splayed over his stomach.

"Let's get you to the toilet." I didn't want to deal with the clean-up if he was sick on the carpet. "Come on." I gently pushed him forward.

I stood back as he knelt in front of the toilet. He took a couple of deep breaths that only resulted in him curling more in on himself before finally throwing up.

Not quite sure what to do, I stood back until he'd finished vomiting.

He sat back once he'd got his breathing back under control, and then lifted his shirt to wipe off his mouth.

My own inhale faltered.

Someone hadn't just done a number on his face. His stomach was *purple*.

Oh my God.

I quickly headed for the bathroom, where I wetted a washcloth, and then went back into the toilet to crouch down in front of him. "Let's get this off you." I pulled gently on the shirt and he slowly and carefully lifted his arms in the air.

His chest wasn't much better off than either his face or his stomach.

I fought my own reflex to throw up as I took in the injuries. "You need to go to A&E."

He shook his head again, but it was weak this time, exhausted. "No. No hospital."

I wiped the washcloth over his face as carefully as I could. "I need to use antiseptic on these scratches." His only answer was a nod. "Come on, let's go to the bathroom."

He sank down to the floor in the bathroom as well. He rested his head against the tub and watched blearily as I went through the cabinets to find what I needed.

He flinched when I pressed antiseptic-dipped cotton to the scratch on his cheek. "Will you tell me who did this to you? If someone attacked you, you need to press charges."

"No police." A startlingly green gaze rose to meet mine. "I'll tell you if you promise not to call the police." His words came out breathlessly, and he curled one arm around his middle. His ribs must be hurting him. I hoped they weren't fractured.

Or worse, broken.

"I promise." I would probably regret it, but what else could I do? I needed to know what had happened to the lad in order to help him.

"It was my dad." He bowed his head again so that all I could see was shaggy auburn hair.

I closed my eyes for a second.

His dad.

How could a father do something like this to his kid? I'd never wanted kids myself, but even if I'd somehow got stuck with one I'd *never* be able to physically hurt another person, like this kid had been hurt.

Green eyes were gazing at me again when I opened mine. "You promised. No police. *Please*."

I stared into his pleading eyes. How could the lad be pleading me to *not* press charges against his father, the one who had hurt him so much? "I know. I promised. I won't."

Tension bled out of him at my simple words, but it was obvious he was still hurting. His laboured breathing and the way his arm still curled around his middle told me loud and clear where he hurt the most.

"How about a bath?" He needed it desperately. He was beat up, bloody, and dirty. "Come on, I'll help you."

I almost had to lift him off the floor to sit on the edge of the tub. I adjusted the water and let it fill.

"Will you be all right on your own from here?" I asked uncertainly. He seemed fairly out of it, but I didn't relish the idea of taking off his clothes. He was a stranger, he was so *young*… it wouldn't be right.

The lad gave a slight shake of his head though and I sighed.

I better not get in trouble for this.

I crouched back down to help him get out of his clothes. I started with the shoes, which I threw in the general direction of the door. Then it was time to rid him of his trousers.

I tried not to look at the skin revealed to me, but it was pretty darn hard to miss the bruises on his legs. They weren't fresh, though, like the ones on his upper body.

These were brown and yellow and I could swear one was the exact same shape as a handprint. It was far up the inside of his thigh.

"Did your dad do this too?" I felt sick and once again had to fight down the urge to throw up.

He gazed down at the handprint bruise. "No, not that one."

"Who did, then?" Did he have more than one abuser in his life?

"I… I don't know."

I could tell he was telling the truth by the way his shoulders drooped and how he refused to meet my eyes again. He seemed ashamed of not knowing.

My God.

I was not fit to deal with this. I was a *chef*, not a counsellor or physician.

I still tried my best not to look as I pulled off his tight boxers, but when he turned to slip into the tub I couldn't help but see the brown and blue bruises on both his arse cheeks as well.

Oh my God…

My stomach clenched tight in anger over the fact that someone could do this to another person, in frustration over the lad refusing me to call the police, and in sadness that he clearly let most of this stuff happen to himself.

"Are you one of Dion's students?" I rose from my crouched position and sat down on the edge of the tub. "What's your name?"

There was a fleeting glimpse of panic on his bruised face and in those green eyes as they flicked up to me before cutting away. "Chad," was the mumbled reply.

Chad…

A bell rang loud and clear in my mind.

Of course, it had to be.

Dion wouldn't have given his home address to just any of his students… except for one.

The one he'd cheated on me with.

I wanted to be angry at being stuck with *that* particular student, but I couldn't be. Not when the lad was in this bad of a shape, when apparently being in such a shape was a regular thing for him.

I couldn't feel anything other than compassion.

"I'm sorry. I'm so sorry." The lad—no, Chad—

bent his head so far his jaw pressed against his collarbone.

"You have nothing to be sorry for." I reached out to switch the water from the tap to the shower head. "Close your eyes."

Those big, brilliantly green eyes.

He did as instructed and I moved the showerhead over him, wetting and plastering his shaggy hair to his head. It must've hurt him to have the warm water hit his bruised and scraped up skin, but he didn't make a single movement.

I turned off the water before I took my own bottle of shampoo and squished some out into my palm, rubbing my palms together a couple of times before I applied it to Chad's hair.

Being very careful, I made sure I got all strands of auburn hair covered. I massaged his scalp gently and I knew I did it right when Chad sighed silently and leant further in against me.

I turned the water on again and rinsed his hair out, and this time Chad did wince when he got shampoo in the scratch on his cheek. I tried to be careful, had even tipped his head back, but a few treacherous drops escaped.

I shampooed his hair another time, as it clearly needed it. I massaged his scalp again too, and he relaxed even more this time around.

"Do you have any other family?" I couldn't fathom how he could have, since clearly nothing had been done about his current situation. Unless they were as abusive as that bastard of a father he had.

"My aunt," he murmured. "But I can't go to her. She doesn't know and she'll call the police on him."

"Would that be so bad?" I could feel how he tensed up under my hands. "Wouldn't it make your life better if he wasn't in it?"

He was silent for a long time and I ran the shower head over him again. "Not by much." The answer came once his hair was free of shampoo and finally clean. "Without him I wouldn't even have a place to live. He provides that, at least."

But if his dad beat him… "Couldn't you live with your aunt, then, if he wasn't around?"

"She doesn't deserve that. I couldn't sponge off her. I've got no prospects. I haven't even got my A-levels."

I frowned.

He hadn't got his A-levels?

Dion hadn't said anything about that.

In fact, Dion hadn't mentioned Chad at all since he'd told me about having cheated.

That was three weeks ago.

"How old are you?" I'd thought the student Dion had cheated on me with had been eighteen, or nearly so, but if Chad had dropped out of college before the end of the year…

It was difficult to tell how old he might be, what with his face swelling up as minutes went by.

But Jesus, what if he was like really *young*?

"Nineteen," was the mumbled reply. "I'll be twenty this December."

My frown deepened.

He was turning twenty?

That didn't make any sense at all.

Had he taken two years off?

Retaken two years?

Or a mix of both?

"I repeated my last year of my GCSEs *and* I had to retake my first year of A-levels, because I failed them both." Another thing he was ashamed off, I could tell. "I just… I couldn't fail anymore, so I quit."

"You didn't quite because of… Dion?" The name came out reluctantly. I'd been so angry at Dion when he'd confessed.

I was still angry at him for cheating on me.

"No." Chad shook his head. "Not really. He tried to help me, you know, before—" He shut himself up, but I knew what he'd been about to say. *Before they'd slept together.* "I'm not book-smart. I couldn't take failing anymore, and… I needed to find work."

I didn't know what to say. I dipped a clean washcloth into the water and, as slowly and as gently as possible, slid it over Chad's bruised and tender skin.

"I needed a job to earn money so I could move out. So I didn't have to live with Dad anymore. So that Harriet doesn't have to worry about me. She doesn't even know anything, really. She just thinks I'm off the rails because of my mum. But she died when I was eleven. It's not like... It's been a long time without her."

"Losing a parent does stay with you. It's not something that's easily forgotten." I hadn't lost my own parents, thankfully, but I would be devastated if I did. Unlike Dion, and Chad, apparently, I had a good relationship with my family.

"I miss her." He hung his head. He was sad and he seemed to need someone to talk to, and I was the only one available. The only one who was nice to him.

"Of course you do." I stroked a hand through his wet hair, ruffling it. I hoped it would soothe him at least a little bit. "I'm going to go find some clothes for you to wear. You just stay here for a bit, okay?"

When he nodded, I stood and went into the guest room.

It had been my room for the past three weeks.

I hadn't shared a bed with Dion since he'd confessed to cheating. Cheating with a *student*.

I'd thought it was such a cliché. Maybe I still did, a little bit, but… Chad was so troubled, he had such a difficult life.

Maybe Dion had felt like I did right now, that he'd wanted to help him out, but then it had somehow escalated.

Or maybe Dion had just fallen for him.

That was always a possibility, after all.

CHAPTER 9

I dug out a pair of joggers, boxers, and a tee from my closet.

They'd be too big on Chad, as he was small and way too thin. I wasn't exactly a big bloke myself, but I was taller and broader and more toned than him.

Chad had the *potential* to fill out more; it was so very clear he wasn't eating healthily, or much at all.

He was in the very same position I'd left him in when I walked back into the bathroom.

I put the clothes down on the counter and bent under the sink to get a big, fluffy towel. "Come on."

He slowly stood up in the tub and braced himself on my shoulder with one hand as he stepped over the edge.

I carefully held onto his side, and then wrapped

the towel around him once he was standing with both feet on the floor.

I dried him off as gently as I could, and then Chad slipped into the boxers and joggers. It took time, as he moved slowly, but he did get them on without help from me. As predicted, they were too big on him, but at least they were soft and clean and comfortable.

After getting a smaller towel from under the sink, I put it over his head and rubbed his shaggy hair dry, before allowing him to put on my tee.

I threw both towels towards the laundry basket and bent to get a new toothbrush from the cabinet next to the one holding the towels. "Here, brush your teeth."

Chad did as he was told, and, after putting on a pair of socks I handed him, he trailed after me into the kitchen.

"I'm making soup. You need to get good, healthy food in you."

He tentatively sat down on a kitchen chair. "You like to cook?"

I smiled at him. "I'd imagine so. I'm a chef." The refrigerator could attest to that as well. It was filled with food. If I didn't do the food shopping, the refrigerator would be decidedly empty.

I pulled out chicken and vegetables and chopped

them up into pieces as the broth simmered on the stove. I added each ingredient as I finished chopping them.

After a brief internal debate, I decided to add some potatoes as well. Chad needed all the nutrients he could get.

I chopped the chicken up last and fried it lightly in a pan before adding it in with the rest. Chicken didn't particularly fit with my vegetable soup, but I felt it was necessary in this instance.

When all was added and I'd washed off everything I'd used including my own hands, I sat down opposite him at the table. It wasn't a big one; there was only enough space for three.

Chad was all but asleep. His eyes kept closing.

"Don't fall asleep yet. You need to eat a little first."

He sat up straighter. "I'm sorry."

I sighed. "You don't have to apologise for everything. You have nothing to apologise *for*."

"But I do." He looked at me. "I *do*."

I stared back into his wide, green eyes. "Nothing's your fault." It really wasn't. Chad wasn't the one who'd cheated. He was not the one who'd had a boyfriend. He was just a kid. Well, maybe not a *kid*, but he was most certainly *young*.

He didn't speak much after that.

He ate slowly when I put a bowl in front of him, but at least he managed to get most of it down.

I was grateful for that. By the time he'd finished eating, he really *was* falling asleep.

I led him into the guest room to what had been my own bed for the last three weeks. He drifted off practically the moment his head hit the pillow and I tucked the covers firmly over him.

I sat on the edge of the bed for a while, watching him sleep.

I hoped he didn't have a concussion. I hadn't considered the fact that he'd been hit in the head, so a concussion might've been a possibility.

Without thinking, I reached out to brush a few strands of still-damp auburn hair away from his face.

My evening certainly hadn't turned out the way I'd thought it would.

I hadn't ever expected to meet Dion's student face to face, and yet here he was sleeping in my bed. I'd cared for him and fed him and let him in my bed... and how could I not have done that? He had been hurt and clearly at the end of his rope.

I couldn't help but like him, either. From what I'd seen so far, he was a sweet lad with his frequent apologies. Very troubled, yes, but sweet. I never would have even imagined that I'd end up *liking* the bloke Dion had cheated on me with, and yet I did.

It didn't make me any less angry at Dion. He was the one who had cheated, after all. I simply couldn't forget that.

For the first time in three weeks, it seemed I would have to share a bed with Dion again.

The two of us felt a lot like strangers lately.

Dion stayed late at college almost every day now, to grade tests or whatever it was he did. I didn't think he stayed late for anything else, or any*one* else. He'd cheated with Chad, yes, but I didn't think he would do so again with someone else.

I usually spent the evenings alone at home, watching the telly. If I had a late shift, which was rare though they did happen, I stayed for as long as possible too.

We were avoiding each other, plain and simple.

I didn't like the current situation. I didn't like it at all, but what could I do? I was angry and hurt, and I couldn't simply forgive Dion for what he had done. I didn't want to lose Dion either, however, and so everything was becoming increasingly difficult to deal with.

Maybe it was time to have that chat with Dion I'd been putting off.

I hadn't wanted to hear a word about the student Dion and cheated with, but as of today… well, Chad was here and he was hurt.

I was fully involved, whether I wanted to be or not.

~

THREE WEEKS earlier I was wistfully unaware of the fact my boyfriend had just cheated on me.

Until he came home, anyway.

If I'd actually looked at him when he came into the kitchen, instead of being too busy with my pots and pans, I would've perhaps been prepared for what was coming.

After two years together, there wasn't anything Dion could hide from me anymore. He might be stoic and silent, but I knew how to read him.

"I'm making a curry for dinner," I told him instead of hello. "Quite a lot of it too, so I hope you're hungry."

"Jeremy."

I froze. Not just because of his flat tone, but because he called me by my full name.

Usually he was content to use the nickname he'd given me, so using my full name wasn't something I wasn't used to anymore.

"Can you leave the curry for a while and come sit down?"

Something was wrong.

Very, very wrong.

I could feel it in my *bones*.

I shut the heat down and left the pot to simmer then sunk down on a kitchen chair.

He'd already sat down, and he had his head bowed. His hair was a bit more ruffled than it tended to be after a day of work. He always kept it carefully combed when he had to work, as he liked to look all professional.

"Windy out?" I tried to joke, wanting to be rid of the heavy atmosphere that shrouded us.

"What?" He looked up, confused.

I waved my hand towards his head. "Your hair. It's all ruffled, like."

Something crept over his expression. Something looking an awful lot like guilt. He'd bowed his head again though, so I couldn't have another look to be sure. "Jeremy…"

"Just spit it out, Dion. Like ripping off a plaster." My body was coiled tight in nervousness.

"I cheated on you."

The words washed over me, leaving me shocked and stunned and *cold*. "You… what? When?"

"Just now. Before I came home." He had his hands clasped, and he held on so tight both were turning white. "With a student."

I didn't think I could feel worse, but that did it.

"A student? Are you losing your job?"

Cheated on me with a student.

Cheated.

With a student.

Cheated.

The words were on repeat in my head and they made me feel numb.

He shook his head. "I'm not, no. Unless he tells, but I don't think he will."

"Know him that well, do you?" It came out in a snarl.

"Better than any of my other students, yeah." It was whispered to the table top.

A sick thought churned in my stomach. "How long's it been going on? How long have you been stringing me along for?"

"What—Jeremy, no!" His head shot up. "It was only today, I swear. I've been kind to Chad—uh, my student—because something's going on with him and I want him to trust in me. I don't think he trusts anyone. But today things got out of hand…" He trailed off.

It was just as well.

I didn't need to hear the end of that sentence.

Though, again, some small masochistic part of me wanted him to go on.

I crossed my arms over my chest and leaned back

in my chair, as far away from him as I could. "How old is he?"

Dion taught Sixth Form college. Sixteen to eighteen year olds, and the odds were in favour of said student being underage as well as his, well, *student*.

"Nineteen going on twenty."

"That's not possible." I shook my head fervently. "Sixteen to eighteen, that's the age of the kids you teach."

"He failed last year."

It was a good thing Dion wasn't a maths teacher. "Then he should be eighteen going on nineteen. You really should get your lie straight before telling it to me."

"Jem." His gaze were begging me to understand. "He's not doing well in school. He failed his GSCEs, had to retake that year, and he failed his first year of A-levels, so now he's retaking that one."

Okay… So. At least he wasn't jailbait.

Another sick thought twisted my stomach. "Are you leaving me for him?"

"No!" It came out instant and fierce. "I would never leave you. I love you."

"Obviously not enough." *Cheated. Cheated. Cheated.* "When you love someone, you don't cheat on them."

Dion finally unclasped his hands, only to run

them through his hair in frustration. "I'm not going to lie, Jem. I have a thing for him. He's sweet, but broken, and he refuses to tell anyone what's wrong. I wasn't going to act on it though, because I really do love you. But when he jumped me today... I couldn't resist." He looked miserable.

As well he should.

I wasn't sure what I felt.

Surely miserable, but also still in shock over the fact that he actually had cheated on me.

I'd thought we were tight, just us. That we were all good and that he wouldn't have had to look other places.

"Is this my fault?" The words tumbled out. "Am I not good enough? We haven't had sex in a while..." It tapered off. I had no idea how to end the sentence, anyway.

"No, that's not it." He shook his head. "What we have means the world to me, Jem."

Could I really believe him? I would have, yesterday.

But after his admission of cheating... obviously it didn't mean enough.

I couldn't face it anymore.

Couldn't face him or what he'd done. I didn't want to hear another word about that student of his.

"Enjoy the curry." I strode out of the kitchen and

into the guest-room, slamming the door shut after me.

I sunk down on the bed and sat for long minutes just staring down at the floor in-between my feet.

That night I went to sleep in that bed and I continued doing it for the next three weeks.

We didn't really speak in those weeks, and it was mostly my fault, but I still couldn't face him cheating on me.

And then I was faced with the student himself falling into my arms.

Fate was a bitch, all right.

CHAPTER 10

*T*he front door squeaked a little as it was opened and then closed.

The hinges definitely needed to be oiled soon.

I added it my mental to-do list as I listened to Dion's steps in the hallway.

"Evening, Jem." Dion's greeting wasn't like it had once used to be; warm and soft. It was hesitant and wary, as if he wasn't even sure he could greet me.

It was thoroughly my fault.

My mood hadn't exactly been the best lately, and I always took it out on Dion. The man I was supposed to love.

What a mess.

"There's soup on the cooker for you." I turned my head to watch Dion's broad back disappear into the kitchen. I pressed my lips together as my thoughts spun, and then I got up and went over to lean in the doorway.

Dion had put the cooker on and was stirring the soup. "You've made a lot."

"Yeah." I glanced over my shoulder towards the guest room. The door wasn't closed properly. I hadn't wanted to close the room off completely in case Chad needed anything. He hadn't exactly been okay when he'd gone to bed, just too tired to deal with anything else.

I watched Dion's profile silently for a few minutes.

He was a couple of inches taller than me and wider through his chest and shoulders. He worked out a lot more regularly than I did, and so he had a tight, fit body.

I should know.

Up till three weeks ago I saw Dion naked every day.

His dark-blond hair was a little longer than usual and it was curling over the collar of his shirt. He looked tired too, and I knew it was also my fault.

"So." I glanced towards the guest room again. "Your student's here. You know, *the* student."

He froze for several seconds before slowly turning around to face me. He looked suspicious, like he didn't believe what he was hearing. "What'd you say?"

"Your student. The red-head you cheated on me with?" I couldn't stop the trace of bitterness and hurt that bled into my voice.

I'd been hurt and angry for three weeks. It wouldn't simply disappear because I'd taken care of the student in question.

It was still *Dion* I was angry with.

"He's here. He's sleeping in the guest room."

His brows drew together in a frown. "Why? Why is he here? Why is he asleep in our guest room?"

"He was beaten halfway into next year." I still couldn't get the sight of Chad's swollen face and his bruised and beaten body out of my mind. "From what I gathered, it's a regular thing."

Dion sighed and closed his eyes. He turned away slightly, but I could still see the worry painted clearly on his face. He still cared for Chad; he still worried about Chad. "It is. When he did show up at college he was usually bruised."

"No one did anything?" I couldn't believe no one had taken action. A student had been abused, and not a single person had done anything to help him?

"He wouldn't admit to anything." Dion tangled his fingers in his hair and pulled slightly in frustration. "I tried to talk to him. The counsellor talked to him. He refused. Said he'd been in fights. We couldn't do anything without him confessing. He was of age. For all we knew he *did* get in fights."

"How long was he your student?" I needed to know. I needed to know how long Dion had seen Chad show up bruised without doing anything about it.

"Only for half a year. He quit three weeks ago."

I was weirdly relieved upon hearing that.

It wasn't much to go by.

There were still other teachers who had seen Chad though in earlier years and who had let his situation pass. I couldn't fathom why anyone would overlook such a blatant display of abuse.

Dion looked pained as he turned back to fully face me. Pained and guilty at the same time. "Why did he come here?"

"He had nowhere else to go." I stared into his brown eyes. "You gave him your home address."

"Yeah, I... I'm sorry." He did look guilty, but I could clearly see the worry for Chad there too.

Something twisted painfully in my stomach.

It wasn't much fun to see my own boyfriend so worried about someone else, someone he'd slept with.

"It's fine," I assured him, but my voice shook slightly. "I helped him. I cleaned him up, I leant him my clothes, I fed him, and I put him to bed. He's going to be hurting for a while, but he'll be fine eventually."

"Thank you." Those two words held a world of meaning. *Thank you for taking care of him. Thank you for not holding a grudge against him. Thank you for helping him after what I did.*

I bowed my head. "I didn't do it for you. I did it for him." I knew those words would hurt him. They were meant to.

I didn't like hurting him, but Dion had hurt me first. It just… I was so petty I couldn't even let it go in the face of the evening's previous events.

Dion turned back to stir the soup. His back was straight and his shoulders tense. "How many times am I going to have to say I'm sorry?"

"Saying sorry doesn't change the fact that you cheated on me, Dion." My eyes stung. I refused to let them fill with tears, though.

I would *not* cry.

I'd cried enough that first week after Dion had told me.

"I broke it off with him. I told you all about it. I come back to you *every* day. Doesn't that mean anything?" He still wouldn't turn back to face me, but I could tell he was upset. I heard it in the tone of his voice.

"It does. But I can also see that you still care very much about him."

Dion didn't say anything to that, neither confirmation nor denial. He might as well have twisted a knife in my gut. I'd never been stabbed before, but I imagined it would hurt equally as much as Dion's pointed silence.

I turned and went back to the sofa. I'd had the telly on mute earlier, my thoughts too loud to be able to focus on anything, but finally I turned it back on.

Better to lose myself in a reality show than to think of the fact that I might just lose Dion completely.

∾

"Jem."

I groaned and tried to slap away the hand shaking me awake.

"Jeremy!"

"What?" I rolled over onto my back and cracked my eyes open. Dion was standing over me, perfectly dressed for work. "I'll see you tonight, Dion." He did *not* have to wake me to tell me he was going to work. He'd never done that before, so why start now when we were hardly on speaking terms?

"He's gone."

I blinked myself further awake.

"What?" I knew I was repeating myself, but I couldn't come up with anything better to say. I'd just woken up; my brain wasn't fully online yet.

I stared up at Dion, who was beginning to look really distressed.

The previous day's events came back to me in a flash, and I pushed myself up on my elbows. "*Gone?*"

"I went into the guest room to check on him before I went to work, and he wasn't there." He kept repeatedly glancing at the doorway. The door was wide open, with a view of the entire living room. "The bed's made. Your clothes are neatly folded on top of it. He's *gone*."

"But…" My brain was still struggling to keep up. "He has nowhere to go."

"Yet he still left." I could tell he was both frustrated and restless. It was in the way he couldn't stand still. "You have to find him, Jeremy."

I pushed myself up into a proper sitting position, incredulous. "*I* have to find him?"

"You've got the day off, right?" He glanced down at me, but he quickly averted his eyes when I met his gaze head-on. "I have to go to work. I can't take a sick day today. There's a faculty meeting."

"I don't know him, Dion. This is London we're living in. I wouldn't even know where to start looking." I ran a hand through my hair, ruffling it even more than it probably was.

"His aunt… She has a café in Soho. *Harriet's Café.*"

I sighed. "He wouldn't go to her yesterday. What makes you think he will today? His face will look even worse than it did last night."

"But she might know where else he'd go." Dion swallowed audibly. "Please, Jem. I beg you. Find him. I don't want him to get hurt any more than he already is."

It hurt to see just how much he cared for Chad.

But it also hurt to think about what could happen to Chad if he went back home, or if he got in another fight, or… a lot could happen.

I didn't want anything to him to him.

Dion was right.

Chad had been hurt enough.

"I'll do my best," I promised.

Dion stared at me for a long moment, looking torn. "Thank you," was all he said, though, and with that he turned and left.

I fell back on the bed with a sigh. *Why did he leave?* I rubbed at my eyes. Hadn't I been clear enough about wanting him to stay last night? I'd wanted him to. I certainly didn't want him to go back to that abusive father of his.

I rolled out of bed and dressed quickly before going into the bathroom to fix myself up.

If there was one thing I was certain of, it was that I couldn't waste any time. Chad wasn't exactly in a good state of mind. He was trapped in a dark spiral of depression. He was clearly self-destructive, since he let all those awful things happen to him.

Something definitely had to be done before the self-destruction ruined him completely.

CHAPTER 11

*I*t was a small café, but it was nice-looking and homey.

There were a few people seated inside, some eating, others sipping tea and reading. Two women were talking animatedly at one of the tables. The long, tumbling red curls of one of them contrasted with the blonde, sleek bob of the other.

"Hi." I stepped up to the counter. A lad—well, man, I suppose, figuring him to be at least eighteen—stood behind it. He had golden-brown hair and wore a pair of wire-framed glasses. "I'm looking for Harriet." I took a gamble that Harriet was indeed her name, hoping she had named the café after herself. Dion hadn't mentioned otherwise.

The lad smiled and leaned to the side a little so he could see past me. "Harriet!" he called softly.

The two women, the blond and the redhead, both turned at his voice. I could take one bet as to who was Chad's aunt, and I was a hundred percent sure I would be right.

"Yes, love?" The redhead stood up from the table and walked over to us.

"He wants to talk to you." The lad nodded to me.

I was taken aback as her green eyes, so very much alike Chad's, settled on me in friendly curiosity. "What can I help you with?"

"I'm looking for Chad. I was hoping maybe you'd seen or heard from him?"

Her smile faltered. "I haven't. What's wrong?" I thought I detected worry in her tone, but I couldn't be certain, since I didn't know her.

"Nothing." At least I hoped there was nothing wrong, besides the obvious. "I just… I need to talk to him, that's all. If you hear anything, could you please let me know?"

She tilted her head to the side, narrowing her eyes at me. "I don't even know who you are."

Well, that was complicated.

"Are you involved with Chad?"

"Ah, no." I shook my head. How could I explain my relationship to Chad to his *aunt*? If she didn't know what was up with his dad, she certainly wouldn't know about Chad and Dion. "It's complicated. Thing is… well, he spent the night at our place last night, but he wasn't there this morning. I just want to make sure he's all right."

She blinked, taking in what I said. "He likes to do that. Disappear, that is." She looked troubled by that fact. "It's really nice of you to care about him. I don't think many do." She smiled sadly.

No, I didn't think so either. "Can I leave you my number?"

She nodded and reached over the counter. I was handed a piece of paper and a pen, and I quickly wrote down both my name and number on it.

"Thank you." I handed it back to her, and then made to leave.

"Wait."

I turned back.

She frowned down at the paper. "He's got a mate. Wynn. He might be there."

Hope fluttered somewhere in my gut. "You know where he lives?"

She nodded and wrote something on another piece of paper then ripped it off and handed it to me. There was a number on it. "If he is there, will you let *me* know?" Her eyes were begging me.

"Of course I will." I read the address. It was in

TT KOVE

Soho, so it wasn't that far from the café. "Thanks." I nodded and left.

If Chad had a friend he could go to, why had he come to us last night? If he had some reason for not going to his friend last night, was there really a chance he would've gone there today?

I found the building and I stood on the pavement looking up at it. I didn't know which floor Chad's friend's flat was in.

Should I go in? See if there were names on the mailboxes or the doors? If I found the right door, should I knock? I didn't know this person—and I didn't want to intrude.

Chad had left… maybe he didn't want anything to do with me.

"That's my flat you're staring at."

I jumped at the cool voice at my side. I turned to find a black-clad, black-haired, black-*eyed* lad standing in front of me. A plastic bag dangled from one hand, overfilled with whatever he'd been shopping.

His gaze took me in stonily. "You need something?" He raised his chin. He seemed challenging.

"I'm looking for someone." I hadn't got a description of Chad's friend. This could be him, he was the same age, but there was also a chance it wasn't him. "His name is Chad."

His already cool eyes narrowed. "What do you want with him?"

So I've got the right lad, at least. "I need to know if he's okay."

"He's far from it, but what's it to you?" He took me in from top to bottom. I couldn't help but feel like he was sizing me up—and I came out lacking. "He's only got one mate, and that's me."

"He spent the night in my flat," was all I was willing to give. "But he was gone this morning."

"He shag you or something?" Now his gaze took on more of a leer as he looked me up and down.

"No." Far from it. "It's not like that."

"Then what's it like?" He crossed his arms over his chest. I didn't know how he managed it while still holding the full bag, but he did. "I'm not giving you shit until you give me something."

What happened to having some faith and trust in other people? "Look, I just want to know if he's okay. If he's with you, clearly he is." If he was this protective over Chad when it came to strangers, he surely was in other aspects too.

"He's not okay. Not at *all*. And he won't be as long as people keep beating him down. Literally and figuratively." His gaze burned into mine.

I had a sinking feeling he wasn't just talking

about Chad's father, but that he knew about Chad's affair with Dion—as well as how that had ended.

"Can you just tell him that we're here for him, if he needs anything? That I did want him to stay, that he didn't have to sneak out in the middle of the night?"

His eyes narrowed further. "Who's we?"

"I'm Jeremy." I splayed my hand out on my chest. "My partner's name is Dion."

He let out a breath and his eyes widened a fraction.

So he does know about Chad and Dion.

"Both of you fucking him over now? Hasn't he had enough after being shagged, and then kicked to the kerb?"

I swallowed the hurt that stabbed my chest. "We're worried about him."

"Sure you are." He snorted and headed for the door.

"We are!" I didn't know why it was so important for me that this *brat* understood—but it was. "He came to us last night. I *helped* him. So I worry about him."

He turned with one hand on the door. "He's with people who actually *do* care about him now. Who won't *fuck* him over. So you can both take your worry and *shove it*. Your boyfriend used him for a quick shag and discarded him afterwards. I won't let the both of you have some twisted three way thing going on, where you'll just shove him out in the cold once you're tired of him. Spice up your own sex-life without involving him in it. He's a good lad, he deserved more than being used and discarded." And with that, he slammed the door.

I stood frozen, eyes locked on the point where he'd just been.

His words repeated themselves in my head, over and over again.

I SAT ON THE SOFA, waiting for Dion to come home.

He'd been worried this morning, so surely he wouldn't stay late tonight.

I tensed up when I heard the door open and shut, and then even more as I heard his footsteps approach.

"Hey." He stopped in the doorway, glancing around uncertainly.

"Hey." I watched him silently for a minute, Wynn's words still on repeat in my head. "Sit down. We need to talk."

He put his briefcase away then came over to sit on

TT KOVE

the other sofa. He bent forward, arms resting on his knees. "You didn't find him?"

"I didn't see him, but I know where he is." *It couldn't be true.* The worry etched on his face right now proved Wynn's words wrong. "What was he to you, Dion? I want the truth. Was he just someone to have some simple fun with? Someone to shag and then forget as you came home to me?"

He drew in a shaky breath, and he wouldn't meet my eyes. "No."

Those words caused both a sharp pain and a flutter of relief. "Were you in love with him?" I could see him press his lips together. "*Are* you in love with him?"

He wouldn't answer, nor look at me. It was answer enough.

"Bloody hell." I hid my head in my hands. "Is this it? The end for us?"

"I love you, you know I do."

"But you love him too." It was *so* obvious.

No answer.

"Why can't you own up to it?" I was angry, all of a sudden. "Fucking own up to it!"

"You really want to hear it, Jem? That I love him? Is that what you *need* to hear?" His voice rose too. "Because I *do*, I fucking love him—and I love *you* and I don't know what the fuck to do anymore!" He got up and started pacing, like he tended to do when he was agitated or frustrated.

The knife twisted in my chest again. "Why'd you choose me?" He had done that. He'd broken it off with Chad and come home to confess everything to me.

He shook his head, still pacing back and forth on the living room floor. "There's a lot between us, Jeremy. And not just the flat, the fact we live together. We have two years of experiences and memories. It's hard to walk away from that."

"So if we hadn't had that… you would've chosen him?"

"No! I… I don't know. He was my student."

"Having a relationship with him would've cost you your job if anyone found out."

"I *know*. It was also one reason I—"

Now I pressed *my* lips together. Hurt and anger warred inside me. "That's why you came back to me? Because you didn't want to lose your *job*? That's why you dumped him?"

"Stop twisting my words!" He finally stopped and faced me. His gaze was stormy. "I chose you because I love you. Because I want to spend the rest of my fucking life with you. What we have is special."

"Clearly not enough," I snapped, "or else you wouldn't have cheated on me!"

He reared back, eyes wide for a moment, then he turned away from me as he rubbed at his face.

Feelings warred inside me.

I was so angry I could hit him because of what he'd done, but at the same time I was happy for Chad that he *had* been something special—that he still was, and yet again sad that he'd been the one who'd been cut off.

It was a mess.

"What can I do to fix this, Jem? Fix us? I'll do anything."

"I don't know. Right now I don't think there's anything you *can* do." I buried my head in my hands again.

He was silent. I eventually heard him walk away, into the bedroom. The door closed softly. Once I knew I was alone, I tipped to the side and curled up on the sofa.

Why does life have to be so bloody difficult?

I WENT BACK to sleep in the guest-room that evening, after lying idly on the sofa for hours just staring at the ceiling.

Dion must've gone to bed without even brushing his teeth, because I hadn't seen him since he'd gone into our bedroom. Or maybe he was still awake and waiting for me to go to bed. That's what I would've done, if I'd wanted to avoid him.

The bed was cold and small and alone. Being back in my own bed for just one night had driven home how lonely the guest-room bed really was.

I tossed and turned for what felt like hours. I wasn't sure it had been hours, but not being able to sleep was a bitch and it always felt a lot longer than it really was.

I must've dosed off though, because next thing I knew I sat straight up in bed as my mobile blared out my ringtone on the bedside table.

My hand fumbled so much the phone fell to the floor, which was carpeted, thankfully, else it probably would've fallen to pieces.

"'lo?" I got out once I finally put it to my ear.

All I could hear at first was sniffling. "J-Jeremy?"

I frowned at the number on the screen for a moment, but it wasn't one I had saved, then put it back to my ear. "Who is this?"

"I'm sorry if I woke you up, but you left your number, so I thought I'd ring you—"

I recognised the voice now. "Harriet?" I sent off a text to her after my encounter with Wynn, so she'd known where Chad was. "What's wrong?" She was clearly crying.

"Chad's in hospital." She sniffled. "I'm in the A&E now, just arrived, but they won't tell me anything!" She broke down, sobbing loudly in my ear.

"Are you alone?" My chest squeezed tightly. In worry for Chad, and for her. She'd seemed like a nice woman, after all.

"N-no, Angie's here."

"Look, we're coming down too, okay?"

"Mhm!" I could picture her nodding, as she was so upset she wasn't be able to make out proper words.

"Just give us half an hour and we'll be there."

I hung up and jumped out of bed.

Only when my phone was dark again did I realise I hadn't even asked what was wrong with Chad. That made me move even quicker and I slammed the main bedroom door open and clicked the light on.

"The hell!" Dion pulled the duvet up over his head. He was always grumpy when he was woken up.

"We have to go to A&E. Chad's admitted to hospital. Harriet just rang me."

A moment of complete, utter stillness—then he was out of bed too.

That drove home just how much he did care about Chad, because Dion was always loath to leave bed once he was in it. Especially if he'd already managed to fall asleep.

There was no time to dwell on it further though. Chad was in hospital, Harriet was crying—which meant that whatever it was had to be bad.

CHAPTER 12

*D*ion all but ran into the waiting room in A&E, but he stopped once he was *actually* inside.

I grabbed his arm and pointed. "Over there." I could clearly make out Harriet's tumbling auburn curls.

She was bent over in a chair with her head in her hands, but I couldn't mistake her for anyone else. Not with that hair.

Beside her was the blonde woman from the café and opposite them sat the black-haired and black-clad bloke who was Chad's friend.

"Harriet." I went over to her, with Dion close behind me. "Thank you for ringing. How is he?"

Harriet lifted her head and there were tear tracks

on her cheeks. Her makeup was completely ruined. "I don't know. They haven't told us anything yet."

"What happened to him?" Dion stepped up at my side. I could hear the distress loud and clear in his voice. Dion was worried—and he was scared. Scared that it was bad, that Chad wouldn't make it.

"Wynn?" Harriet looked over at the young lad who had completely thrown me off earlier in the day.

He was pale and his lips were pressed together tightly, eyes dark as he looked up at us. "He had too much to drink." He quickly looked away, his head turning sharply to the side.

I turned to see what he was looking at.

A woman had entered the waiting room, and she frantically looked around until she caught sight of Wynn.

"Wynn!" She came hurrying over, clad in a red coat with high stiletto heels on her feet.

Wynn stood. His lips had tightened further and his eyes were hard. "You have no right to be here."

I took a step back, wanting to get out of the crossfire, only to bump into Dion, who somehow once again was behind me.

He grabbed a hold of my shoulders to steady me, and ended up leaving his hands there.

I didn't really mind.

It felt good to have Dion's hands on me again.

"Don't waltz in here and act like you suddenly care about him." Wynn walked closer to her. He was a head taller and he used it to his advantage to loom menacingly over her. "You don't, so stop pretending."

She took a step away from him, her mouth drawing down into a pout. "I do care about him. Madison's my *son*!"

I shook my head in confusion.

Chad was not the only one admitted to hospital?

I glanced back at Dion, who seemed to share my confusion.

When I turned back, I saw a doctor heading our way, looking grim.

My chest constricted, and I felt Dion's hands tighten almost painfully on my shoulders.

"Are you the family of Madison Sisco?"

"I am his mother." The red-clad woman turned around to face the doctor. "How is he, doctor, will he —" She clapped a hand in front of her mouth after taking in the man's expression. "No. No…"

"I am sorry." The doctor bowed his head slightly in what was supposed to be sympathy, but he seemed to be kind of detached. "He didn't make it. There was nothing we could do for him."

"No!" She stumbled back, right into Wynn, who snarled and pushed her away. She stumbled again, only steadying thanks to the quick reflexes of the doctor. She turned and her eyes were cold as they locked on Wynn. "You bastard! You killed him!"

"No, you did." Wynn clenched his jaw shut. "Everything is your fault, you bloody slag." He stepped forward, crowding into her space, and then shoved her again. "You're not wanted or needed here so bugger off. You fucking cunt."

"Wynn!" Dion's hands left my shoulders and he brushed past me to grab a hold of Wynn before he could hurt the slight woman. "Come on, Wynn, calm down or they'll have you tossed out." He seemed familiar with the lad.

Was he, or had he been, one of Dion's students too?

Wynn fought against Dion's grip until Dion was forced to let him go. Wynn didn't go back to attacking the woman—instead he rounded on Dion. "What are you doing here? You fucked Chad over, you have no *right*. It's your bloody fault he's here in the first place."

Dion took a deliberate step back. I could see the anger and guilt fighting for dominance in him.

"Wynn, stop it!" Harriet had stood too now. "Just please *stop* it!" Her tears fell again. She didn't even bother to wipe at them. "I know you're hurting, but please … don't take it out on him. He's here because he cares. That's why we're *all* here. Please."

Wynn stared at her, and then he strode over to drop into the chair furthest away from us. He kept his head turned away from the red-dressed woman, Madison's mother, who was still facing the doctor.

"My son... What happened to him?"

"A combination of an overdose and alcohol poisoning, is the preliminary cause. He had passed even before they brought him in."

Oh my God.

I ran my hand over my face, and then cast a glance over at Wynn, who was still steadily staring at the wall. I thought I could see blankness in his eyes.

"Please, can I see him?"

The doctor nodded, and with a last look at the rest of us, he led her away.

I went over to sink down onto the seat Wynn had abandoned, right across from Harriet's empty seat.

Dion was left standing, and he started to pace restlessly.

I watched him sadly. He was so worried about Chad—it was clear as day for everyone to see that Dion *loved* the kid. He wasn't even a kid, but in his very last teenage year. He was going to be twenty— all grown up.

"Come on, love, sit down." The blonde woman

guided Harriet back to her chair and gently seated her on it.

"I hate waiting." Harriet glanced anxiously towards the doors. "I just want to know how he's doing."

"Waiting is a good thing." The blonde woman held tightly onto Harriet's hands. "That means they're still working on him. They're still saving him."

"God, Angie, I hope so." Harriet drew her hands out of the blonde woman's grip and buried her face in them. She'd stopped crying, though she seemed even more scared and nervous than she'd been before.

I averted my eyes from them. "Dion, come sit down." I couldn't watch him pace any longer.

He only shook his head.

"Wynn…" Harriet's voice brought my attention back to her. "Wynn, I'm so sorry for your loss."

He didn't reply. He sat stonily on the furthermost chair, not moving a muscle. It was impossible for me to know his feelings, but judging from his earlier reaction… well, he must be hurting *a lot*.

"Can you tell me what happened?"

It took several moments, but Wynn finally did turn his head to look at Harriet. "He'd had too much to drink, I already told you this."

"Yes, but…" Harriet shook her head in frustration. "What *happened*?"

"I don't know!" Wynn turned his head away again. "He'd had too much to drink and I was trying to take the bottle from him when… when Madison —" His voice broke off in a shaky intake of breath. "I couldn't wake him up, he was just lying there lifeless, and then suddenly Chad collapsed behind me. The bottle I'd tried to take from him earlier broke and he fell into the mess, choking on his own vomit before he passed out too. I couldn't… I couldn't *do* anything!"

"The doctor said Madison died from an overdose. Did you give him the drugs, Wynn?"

He shook his head. "No."

"But you have given him drugs before, haven't you?" Harriet bent forward. "Both to Madison *and* to Chad."

Wynn pressed his lips together. Then he nodded. "Yeah."

It was Harriet's turn to draw in a sharp breath. "Never again, Wynn. You hear me? *Never* again!" I noticed how her hands shook in her lap. "I want him to get well, and he can't do that if he's under the influence of drugs and alcohol. It has to *stop*."

"It's the only thing he has!" Wynn snapped.

"What?" Harriet looked lost.

I felt dread settle like lead in my stomach. I knew where Wynn was going with this, I knew Chad's wishes on the matter, and I knew what devastating truth she'd have thrown at her.

"Have you ever wondered *why* he's so off the rails? His dearest *mum* might be the underlying problem, but it's not even half of it."

"What are you talking about?" Harriet straightened, green eyes wide as she kept her gaze trained on Wynn.

"You should take a long look at his face later."

"Wynn—" I began warningly.

Harriet was a sweet woman who seemed to really care about her nephew. To have Wynn throw Chad's secrets, which he had hidden from her with great care, in her face like that… I wasn't so sure it was the right thing to do.

It was inevitable for Chad's secret to stay that way, Harriet would very soon find out, but to have Wynn spit them out there in such a cold, cruel tone wasn't right.

Wynn ignored me. "Have you rung daddy dearest yet?"

"He doesn't answer his phone." Harriet took out her own from her purse to check it.

"Just as well. Wouldn't want him to come here and finish what he started."

"What are you hinting at, Wynn?" I could tell Harriet was becoming agitated from the way she suddenly couldn't seem to sit still.

"His favourite pastime is to use his son as his own private punching bag." Wynn delivered the blow in a low, cold voice. "And you are too clueless to notice it. Always have been."

Harriet's phone clattered to the floor as her hands shot up to cover her mouth. "No, that can't be true." She shook her head.

Wynn raised his eyebrows mockingly. "Oh, really? How would you know? Are you the one he comes to when he's just got the crap beat out of him? I think not. That would be *me*. Because I'm the only one who bothers."

"I love him." Tears welled up in her eyes. Her very sincere eyes. "I will do anything for him."

"I guess it's never too late to start," Wynn snapped angrily.

I looked to the blonde woman—Angie?—who I guessed had to be Harriet's girlfriend.

She glanced between Harriet and Wynn with narrowed eyes. She seemed worried about Harriet and angry at Wynn.

I supposed she had every reason to be, as Harriet's partner.

Wynn had just told them Chad's secret, the one

he'd so badly wanted to keep hidden. He'd wanted so much to keep it from his aunt that he'd come to *our* flat instead of going to her.

Dion's pacing stopped, which brought my attention back to him. He was standing still next to my chair, but his eyes were trained behind my back.

I turned around only to have my stomach clench in anxiety as I saw a white-coated doctor heading towards us.

He looked grim.

CHAPTER 13

"What are you really doing here?"

My eyes fluttered open at Harriet's low question. She stood at my side, looking down at me.

I sat up straighter in the uncomfortable chair to give her my full focus. "How is he?"

Harriet had been in to see Chad for the past half-hour.

"Stable. He'll be fine, eventually. At least physically." Harriet sunk down on the chair next to mine.

Angelina, correctly Harriet's girlfriend as I'd had confirmed earlier, was still sat opposite me.

"What do you mean?" I blinked. I'd been on the verge of falling asleep right there in the waiting room.

"He doesn't want to stay with me." She sighed heavily and tilted her head back to look at the ceiling. "I don't know what I've done wrong."

"I don't think you've done anything wrong." I tried to reassure her, but I also honestly believed it. "I think it's more that he doesn't want to involve you in his issues. That he doesn't want to put you in a position where you have to deal with them."

Harriet tilted her head to the side so she could look at me again. "Your boyfriend just went in to see him. It seems like there is—"

"I know," I interrupted her. "I know." I tried for a reassuring smile, but I had a sneaky suspicion it came out more wary.

"Oh no." Harriet sighed and averted her eyes. "What has he done?"

"It's not his fault." I was quick to defend him. Because it was true. Chad had not been the one with a boyfriend at home. That was all on Dion. He'd had me and yet he'd chosen to sleep with Chad.

"That can't be easy for you. I don't know why you're even here." Her perfectly shaped eyebrows drew together in a frown. "I don't think I would've been. I know it sounds spiteful, but… it's true."

"He's very troubled and I want to help him." Since Chad had shown up at my door the evening before… Had it really only been a day? It felt a lot longer. "If he doesn't want to go stay with you, he can come with us."

Harriet's expression changed into one of shocked surprise. "Would you do that for him? What makes you think he'll even go with you when he's refusing to go with me?"

"He came to us yesterday." I'd already told her so, back at the café. I wouldn't say anything else on the subject, but I could tell from her expression that she understood *why* Chad had shown up at our place. "I'll make it clear to him that he's welcome to stay with us. I might not have made it perfectly clear yesterday, which I guess is why he left."

"You're kind." She reached out to squeeze my forearm. "Thank you."

"I won't let him go back to his father." I squeezed her hand in return. "I promise I won't let him go back there."

She nodded gravely. "I... I had no idea. When Chad's out of here, I'm going to have a chat with Bryce. I can't believe—" She shook her head while wearing a far-away expression.

"I'm going to go check on him." I glanced at Angelina as I stood, tightening my grip around Harriet's hand one last time.

She nodded, and when I walked away, she took my abandoned seat.

It didn't take me long to find the room Chad had been assigned. The door was wide open and I peered inside, hoping it was indeed the right room.

Dion was in a chair next to the bed, with Chad's limp hand clasped between his own.

Chad himself was asleep. He'd just had his stomach pumped, so it was definitely best for him to stay asleep for a while still. He looked small and fragile in the bed. His auburn hair was a mess, his freckled face pale where it wasn't discoloured from bruises. He was in a hospital gown with a thick duvet pulled up to his chest. His arms were pale and thin, a testament to the fact that he didn't have a healthy diet.

Dion's elbow rested on the bed as he held Chad's hand. He was bent over slightly, his eyes never leaving Chad's face. I felt pain stab my chest at the sight and I wasn't quite sure what caused it. Jealousy, hurt, frustration, worry… maybe a mix of all of them.

Dion's obvious feelings for Chad hurt me and they did make me jealous.

But Chad's entire situation made me both frustrated and worried. I wanted to help him, no matter what my feelings were about Chad's connection to Dion.

"Jem." Dion dropped Chad's hand the moment

he caught sight of me in the doorway. He looked torn and miserable.

"It's okay." I walked over to him and put both my hands on Dion's shoulders.

He hesitated for a moment, but he did pick Chad's hand up again. He stroked his thumb over the back of it before turning it around. The palm of Chad's hand was bandaged.

I remembered what Wynn had said earlier, about Chad falling into the shattered mess of the bottle. The glass must've cut up his palms, hence the bandage.

"All I ever wanted was to help him," Dion muttered. "I royally messed that up, didn't I? And in the process I messed up you and me."

I bent down to nuzzle against his coarse hair. "You can have your second chance at helping him now," I murmured. "He's refusing to stay with Harriet, so we're taking him home. We're going to help him. You and I, together."

Dion tensed. "Why would you do that?"

"Because I feel sorry for him. Because he has a crappy life and he sees no way out of it." I wrapped my arms loosely around Dion's neck, and then looked down at Chad's bruised, swollen face. "Because you care for him, Dion, and I care about you."

One of Dion's hands covered mine. "I am so sorry for hurting you, Jem, but… thank you."

I smiled against his hair, but I knew it was a bitter one. "I've been hurting you for the past three weeks. I think we should stop hurting each other now." Honestly, I was afraid I'd be giving a whole lot more than that.

The worry gnawed at me, the worry that I would eventually lose Dion… lose him to Chad.

And I didn't know if I could, if I *would*, fight it, because Chad had such a miserable life and he deserved to be happy. If Dion was what made him happy then maybe I would have to let Dion go.

If it came down to it, I hoped I could do it, but I wasn't sure. I loved Dion *so* much, and I did want him for myself even after recent happenings, so it was hard not to be selfish about it.

But Chad deserved happiness too, and if the current situation only made all three of us more miserable… well, I was pretty sure I would be the one to suffer in the end.

Visiting hours hadn't even started yet, and now that we knew Chad would be okay, only direct family were allowed to stay in hospital outside of those hours.

So Dion and I went home, where we spent the morning in tense silence.

I made breakfast for the both of us, while he sat at the table, worrying and fretting silently.

"I don't understand why he won't let his aunt help him," Dion said once I put two plates on the table and sat down opposite him. "Why let *us* help, when she's right there and willing? She knows him a lot better than we do."

I studied him. "When you left home, was there anyone outside your immediate family you turned to?"

"No." I hit a sore spot, apparently. "But my extended family *knew* what went on in my home. Harriet didn't. They turned a blind eye—she was unaware. She knows now and she's not going to let it go."

I shook my head as I stared down at my food. "I don't know, Dion. I've always had my parents. They're good, loving people who've never hurt me. They wouldn't dream of ever hurting me. I have no idea how his mind works. I don't think he's even off a right mind, at the moment."

"You saying you think he's mental?" Dion raised

his eyebrows challengingly, and I was startled at the fierce protection in his voice.

I held my arms up, palm out. "No. I think he's depressed. But coming from that childhood, who can blame him?"

Dion stared at me then hung his head as he dragged a hand over his face. "I wish I could've done more for him. Before it turned into *this*."

I wasn't sure if he meant the state of his relationships, with Chad and me, or Chad's general situation. Maybe both.

"Well, he'll be staying for a while now. You can make it up to him."

Dion lifted his head up again, gaze boring into me. "Are you doing this just for me? Is it something you're *really* okay with?"

"I'm doing it for both of you." My heart broke inside my chest. "He loves you. He trusts you. And you love him."

He was silent, frozen in place.

"Maybe we could try… I don't know. An open relationship?" I twiddled my thumbs. "Just you and him, I mean. I love you, he loves you, and you love us both, and I don't want to lose you, Dion."

"I *chose* you."

It was my turn to look down at my folded hands. I couldn't meet his eyes. "I know. But I think you might choose him given time, and I don't want to lose you. So there's another opportunity, and I'm grabbing at it."

"We haven't been together in three weeks, Jem. How's this going to help? You can't get over me being with him—and you shouldn't either, because I *did* cheat on you, and I regret that so much. But what you're proposing now… you really think that's going to make it any better?"

"I don't know. It's a possibility. We can try it out." I wasn't sure why I was even talking. Why was I suggesting for him to be with Chad as well as with me? He was right. That couldn't possibly make me feel better. "I'm tired of being hurt and angry—I'm tired of punishing you. I want things to change."

I stood, abandoning my food, and went over to him. I ran my hands over his broad shoulders then pushed his chair out from the table a bit so I could straddle his lap. I didn't meet his surprised gaze, instead I ran my hand over his slightly stubbled skin.

"I've missed touching you. Missed *us*." I leaned in to nuzzle his cheek. He smelled faintly of cologne and it was such a damn *familiar* smell. It brought another kind of ache to my chest. "I miss you."

His hands settled on my back hesitantly, as if he wasn't sure if he was allowed to.

I couldn't blame him for being hesitant—I'd been

a right moody tosser the last three weeks. "I miss you too. More than you know."

I put my forehead on his shoulder to gather myself. Hurt and bitterness and anger still warred inside me, but there was also a feeling of content-ment, brought on by finally being so close to my boyfriend again, of feelings his strong arms around me.

I had a sudden need to cry, but I fought it because doing so would be too humiliating.

Chad had reason to cry.

Dion, too, because he was drawn between us.

But me, my problems didn't seem so big in the grand scheme of Chad's crappy life.

"Jem."

"Don't say anything." I grabbed onto his neck tightly.

"But—"

"We'll figure it out. In time, we'll figure it all out." I had to believe we would. Forgiveness wasn't coming easily to me, but we could try to move past it. We could try to reconnect.

Sharing a bed was a must from now, with Chad coming to stay with us. Maybe... just maybe, we could reconnect in all kinds of ways.

I wanted it *so* much. I wanted it to happen—but I wasn't sure I could allow it to happen.

The fact that he'd been with someone else, even someone as sweet and broken as Chad, was a difficult thing to get over.

But I wanted to try—I needed to try—because I loved him.

I'd never loved anyone the way I loved Dion—and I needed to keep him, no matter what.

CHAPTER 14

When we got back to the hospital, now under visiting hours, we found Chad alone in his room. Both Harriet and Angelina were absent.

"Hey." Dion strode right over to the bed and took one of Chad's thin hands in his.

Chad peered up at him blearily.

He blinked a few times.

He must have been be on some kind of drug, since he didn't seem to be completely himself just yet. I didn't know what kind of drugs they gave after pumping one's stomach—or if they even gave any at all.

It seemed a bit counter-effective to administer drugs when a person had just been pumped and treated for alcohol poisoning, but then again… surely he must've got something for the pain?

I assumed it must be painful anyway.

Chad swallowed several times, seemingly unable to get his voice to work.

Dion handed him the glass on the bedside table, and Chad took a couple of small sips.

I hovered by the door, uncertain now.

Should I leave them to talk? I was just as involved as Dion was now—or no, not *quite* as involved as he. I hadn't had my dick in the lad, after all.

Bloody hell, Jeremy, I berated myself. This was not a time to be bitter and angry.

Chad was hurt. He needed warmth.

I took a step closer so I stood at the end of his bed.

Chad's gaze flitted over me briefly, but was soon drawn back to Dion.

"How are you feeling?" Dion only had eyes for him.

I couldn't lie, it made my heart ache a little bit.

"Weak." Chad swallowed again and Dion held the glass out, but he shook his head this time.

"Where's your aunt?"

"I told her to go home." His voice became stronger by the minute. "She has a business to run. It's not like I need her here."

His words were tough—but even I could tell it

was all a front. He looked like a scared little kid in that bed. Even his freckles—not to mention bruises —were pale.

Dion's free hand, the one not holding Chad's, stretched out, hesitated the briefest moment, then he ran his fingers down Chad's cheek lightly. "You scared me to death."

Chad's eyes narrowed. "Like you care." He turned his head the other way, but I took notice of how he didn't try to extricate his hand from Dion's.

"I do, Chad. I really do. You've been out of school for three weeks—"

"I quit."

"So they tell me, yeah. Why did you do *that*? Because of me?"

Chad shrugged. An awkward thing to do while lying in bed, but he managed it. "No." A lie there if I'd ever heard one. "I'm too stupid for college. Better find something to do where I can actually earn some money."

I could understand him wanting to earn his own money, especially when living in an abusive home. Of course he wanted to get away from it, and if he couldn't manage school then it wasn't worth it getting his arse kicked by his own dad every day.

Not that I knew it happened every day, but it certainly happened often.

"Why are you refusing to go with Harriet?" I put my hand down on the railing of the bed. The metal was cold, but the grip grounded me. "You want to go back to your dad?" Who refused to go with the aunt who clearly cared to go back to the abusive father?

The corners of his lips pointed downwards in a miserable expression. "She doesn't deserve my shit."

"But she wants it." Maybe I should've denied the *shit* part, but it was better to get my point across. "She wants you to live with her."

"I can't do that to her!" he shouted, and then subsided into quiet misery.

Dion squeezed his hand tight. "You're coming home with us then. I'm not letting you go back to your dad. No way."

Chad turned his head slowly, gaze raking over first me then Dion in suspicion. "Why would you do that?"

"Because I care about you. I don't want you to go back to that, Chad. You deserve a lot better than being your dad's punching bag."

"What do you know about that?" he muttered, head turning away again. "I'm not worth your attention. Especially not *yours*."

The last part was directed at me, even if he wasn't looking at me. But then he wasn't looking at either of us.

"I'm not going to leave you out on the streets, Chad," I told him quietly. "I can separate my feelings." I glanced at Dion, to find him looking at me too.

Separate feelings…

Maybe that's what he had?

Separated his feelings between me and Chad?

Maybe he didn't even feel the same way about us, two completely different things.

Chad was obviously someone he cared about, someone he worried about, someone who needed someone to be kind to him.

And I was… what was I? I was the partner, the one with my head on straight, so to speak.

Chad and I were nothing alike, yet he cared about both of us.

"I can't." It came out a whisper I almost didn't catch because I was so deep in thought. But I did catch it and it made me frown. "You have no idea how little I can separate mine."

I had a feeling he wasn't talking about the same as I'd been thinking about. He'd only just met me, so there couldn't be a lack of separation of feelings there.

I'd only met him too, for that matter, but the lad I saw in front of me right now wasn't the one Dion had cheated on me with, but a broken young man who needed all the help he could get.

If I could contribute to helping him back on his feet, I would gladly do it. No one should have as miserable a life as he had. It wasn't right, though I knew people had it a lot worse too.

I didn't even want to think about that. Better to think about what I could do here and now for this lad.

"I'm not right in the head," he continued, still trying to get us to back out. "I have terrible mood swings."

"If you quit the drugs, the mood swings will go too," Dion commented drily. "Surely you know the effects of the drugs you use?"

My eyebrows rose.

Drugs?

Chad peered at Dion again, frowning, and then yet again turned away. I didn't know him well enough to read the look on his face.

"Please, Chad. Come with us."

"If you insist," he edged, but I could tell now he *did* want to come with us. Just for Dion or to get away from his dad, I wasn't so sure about though. Maybe a mix of both.

"I *am* insisting."

I knew he'd agree. He had no other place to go, after all.

"Could you—I mean… Can you please go home and get me some proper clothes?" His voice was low, small. "I don't want Harriet to do it. I don't want her to see the state of the house, or Dad to be angry at her if he's in a nasty mood and she shows up alone."

He had a point there.

I wouldn't want her to go there by herself either. I didn't know what Chad's dad looked like, but a full-grown man could easily take petite Harriet, especially if he was angry.

"We will," Dion promised him, squeezing Chad's hand between both of his.

I felt a stab of longing. It'd been over three weeks since he'd properly touched me now. I wanted that again.

But would it happen with Chad around?

I wasn't so sure, but we had to help him. There was no way about it—he needed someone to get his life back on track.

And for now, we were those someones.

I LOOKED up at the house. It wasn't big, and it was right in the middle of the row of houses that flanked this side of the street. All houses were in red brick. There was nothing outside that showed any hint of what I was afraid of finding on the inside.

Dion walked resolutely up to the front door and pressed the bell hard.

"If the man's here, don't do anything stupid," I cautioned as I went up to stand beside him. "We're just here to get Chad's things, nothing else."

Dion cast me a dark look. "This sod should be tossed in jail." He pressed the bell angrily again. "I can't believe no one's ever done something. These are terraced houses. Surely the neighbours on both sides must've known what was going on." He pressed the bell a third time, and this time he held it for much longer. "If I'd known it was his dad back when he was in college, I would've called the police, no matter his protests."

"That's exactly what he *didn't* want to happen."

He started knocking furiously on the door. "I don't understand why he's protecting him."

"He's his father," I murmured.

Dion hadn't had anything to do with his family since he was sixteen years old and had run away from home. He'd never told me exactly what had been going on, but I knew it had been bad. It had to have been for Dion to cut his entire family off completely. Maybe he'd gone through much of the same as Chad?

"That obviously still counts for something."

Dion only shook his head in exasperation. "It doesn't seem like he's here." He tried the knob, and, to both our surprises, the door swung open.

The smell of stale alcohol seeped out and my nose wrinkled.

"Bloody hell." Dion glanced at me, as if to make sure he wasn't alone, then he stepped inside.

I took a deep breath of the fresh air outside before following him. The smell was even worse on the other side of the threshold.

"I can see why he didn't want his aunt to come here." There were stairs to our right and three wide-open doors on the ground floor leading to what seemed to be the living room, kitchen, and toilet. Empty bottles cluttered the floor. There was regular beer, but also stronger stuff like vodka and whiskey.

"Come on." Dion angled his head towards the stairs.

We made our way up slowly. Bottles littered the stairs too, and the upstairs hallway. All the doors were open wide. There were two bedrooms and a bathroom. The closest bedroom had bare walls and were scattered with more bottles, and I assumed this was the father's room.

We both entered Chad's room somewhat hesitantly. It was cleaner than the rest of the house, but only barely. Clothes were strewn about, some clean, some obviously dirty. The walls were completely bare; there was not a single picture or poster.

Dion headed over to the closet. He opened the double doors and peered inside.

I watched as he fished out a bag from the bottom of it, hidden underneath several layers of clutter.

"Should we bring anything other than clothes?" I gathered together a few papers scattered over the desk. They were more pamphlets than papers, actually. The one on top was about depression, the next one about schizophrenia. The last one I gathered was about dyslexia. "Is this the reason he never did well in school?" I waved the last pamphlet in Dion's direction.

Dion looked at it. "I don't know. It's what I thought. I wanted to have him tested, but then... well, then he quit."

Yeah, Chad had quit all right, right after Dion had made it clear to him they were over.

I could read Dion like an open book, so I could clearly see the guilt raging inside him again before he turned back around.

"You shouldn't feel so guilty." My voice was low, quiet.

"Really? I developed feelings for him, I shagged him, and then I hurt him. I hurt *you*. I don't want to hurt either of you, and yet that's what I'm still doing."

My heart broke a little.

Yes, Dion *had* hurt me. I'd hurt him in return too, by being angry and resentful at him for three weeks. By moving into the *guest* room. But who *wouldn't* have done that? He'd *cheated* on me.

I hadn't been able to stomach sharing a bed with him. I hadn't done anything wrong in that, had I? Not when Dion was the one who'd done something wrong in the first place.

But Don had been hurt too because he'd had to make a choice. He'd chosen *me*, but that didn't mean it hadn't still hurt him to let Chad go. It was so very obvious it had hurt. That it *still* hurt.

"It's okay, Dion." It wasn't, really. "It's not like you can control how you feel." That was certainly true. I didn't like it, but it was true. "Let's hurry so we can get out of here. I don't like this place." The whole house smelled rank and I desperately felt like taking a shower.

"There's no system in here." Dion looked around. "I don't know what to bring."

I gathered up the clothes scattered around the room. I reckoned, since they were scattered about in this way, that Chad had used them. I didn't bother folding them before putting them in the bag Dion held open though, as I'd wash them when I got home. "Take something from the closet too."

Dion did as instructed and stuffed the bag as full as he could get it.

I, meanwhile, checked out the shelves and drawers on the desk. There wasn't much in them. Nothing Chad would miss, anyway.

I went over to the nightstand. A mobile and its charger were the first things I saw. I took them out and noticed the assortment of condoms in all kinds of colours. There were a couple of tubes of lube, too. Both were half-empty.

I shut the drawer quickly. "Are you ready?" I turned to face Dion, who was zipping the bag shut.

He nodded and led the way out of the room. We went back downstairs and I was about to shut the door after us when a sound registered. "Do you hear that?" I turned back around.

"What?"

"A sound…" I ventured further down the hall-way. There was definitely a sound coming from ahead.

Dion follow behind me.

I stepped over the threshold into what I'd

guessed correctly earlier to be the living room. The smell was even worse in here and I grimaced.

The cause of the sound was the telly.

I glanced around. Why would the man leave the telly on? Why would he even leave the house unlocked? He lived in London; it was definitely ill-advised not to lock your own door.

"Jem." Dion grabbed a hold of my jacket-sleeve. His eyes were trained on the floor in front of the telly. I followed his line of sight. A pair of feet, clad in dirty socks, peeked around the sofa.

Dion dropped Chad's bag and went over to check.

I followed slowly, more unsure.

It was a man lying there, lifeless on the floor. He was on his stomach, so I couldn't see anything other than the matted hair and the dirty clothes. There were flies curling around him and the smell was *foul*.

I stepped back again and covered my mouth and nose with my arm.

"No pulse." Dion straightened up and took out his mobile. "He's cold and completely stiff. He's been here a while, I'd reckon."

I turned away, horrified, as Dion called and informed the emergency serves of the current situation.

Chad must've cared for the man, no matter what

he had done, since he wouldn't call the police on him.

And after everything, after almost dying himself, we'd have to inform Chad that his father was dead.

That could certainly lead to catastrophe.

PART III
CHAD

CHAPTER 15

*T*groaned as I changed position on the bed. My whole body ached and my head thudded painfully. The ache in my body was due to the injuries, but my head was all thanks to the alcohol.

My throat was sore and raw after the tube I'd apparently had in it that had pumped the contents of my stomach.

I couldn't believe I'd had alcohol poisoning.

I'd been drinking for *years* and I'd never suffered from it before.

I had almost died... I hadn't meant for it to happen, but I wished it had. If I'd died, I wouldn't be feeling like this, so bloody worthless.

Madison... he was dead.

I foggily remembered how he'd been passed out on Wynn's bathroom floor. How Wynn had slapped his face and called his name.

Next thing I knew, I choked and glass pricked into my skin.

I lifted my hands. My palms weren't so bad off. The cuts were many, but they were small and not very deep. They would heal before anything else on me did.

Madison.

Madison was *dead*.

I had a hard time believing it. How could he be dead? I'd seen him before finding him in the bathroom and he'd been *fine*.

Well, as fine as Madison could ever have been, which wasn't very, but still. Dead? He hadn't been speaking about death last night, like he'd done earlier in the day.

"I found your picture."

My head snapped around and I groaned loudly in pain at the sudden movement.

When I could focus again, I saw Wynn standing next to my bed.

He held out the aforementioned framed picture and I took it with shaking hands.

"Thanks." I cradled the picture close. I'd have to give it back since I was going to stay with them.

I couldn't believe that either, that Jeremy had *insisted* I go stay with them. I hadn't been able to refuse.

Where else would I go after all?

Only thing I did refuse was going with Harriet.

Wynn looked much like normal. Dressed up all in black.

"How are you?" I tried to get a feel of his feelings, but it was impossible. Wynn kept his emotions well-hidden and not even I, as his best friend, could read him properly. "I'm so sorry, Wynn."

"It's not your fault." He looked down at me. "You didn't give him the alcohol and the drugs. *I* did. I told your aunt I didn't give it to him that time, but I did." His voice broke a little at the end, betraying his feelings. "It's my fault he's dead. It's all my fault."

"No, Wynn—"

"It is." His eyes were a shade darker than normal. "It's my fault. I essentially killed him."

I highly doubted that. "What did you give him?"

"Only poppers. But I overheard the doctor telling Madison's mum that he *swallowed* them. Madison knows that's fatal. That wanker said it was down-right suicide. That Madison killed himself."

I looked down and away. "Madison never seemed happy, you know. If he did it on purpose... it doesn't really surprise me." Madison couldn't exactly be described as being of a sound mind.

I thought about death a lot, but I never spoke about it like Madison had.

"Is that supposed to be my fault too?" Wynn snapped.

"No. I think you did what you *could*. I'm not blaming you, Wynn. Not at all. I just think that there was something seriously wrong with Madison that couldn't be fixed." I kind of felt like that about myself too. Like there was something wrong with me that couldn't be fixed—like I was broken.

"That how you feel about me too, is it?" Wynn was on the verge of exploding and I didn't know how to stop it.

Movement at the door caught my attention, and when I turned my head to look past Wynn, I caught sight of Dion and Jeremy.

My stomach dropped momentarily only to have butterflies start fluttering around in the next second. I always had that reaction when I saw Dion; had since the first day I'd entered the classroom to find him as the teacher.

And Jeremy... Jeremy'd been nice to me. They were still nice to me, both of them.

I tried for a smile, but it didn't quite work out. My

face was swollen and bruised and the movement pulled my skin painfully.

And besides, no matter how nice they were, life still sucked and I honestly wished it could've just ended last night.

They didn't smile back either, so maybe they hadn't even seen my attempt. They looked rather grim.

Maybe they don't want me to stay with them after all.

"Chad…" Dion stepped further into the room. He had the strap of my bag over one broad shoulder.

I took in the frown on both their faces and my stomach dropped again.

This time, though, it was for an entirely different reason.

I tensed up, my whole body going rigid. Whatever they had to tell me, it wasn't good.

Please don't turn me away.

Please, please, please.

If they turned me away, I wouldn't have any other choice than to go with Harriet, and she didn't know the first thing about how to deal with me… I could hurt her, and I would never forgive myself if I did.

Dion and Jeremy were two full-grown men, they could take whatever I dished out, but Harriet… she couldn't. I knew myself well enough not to trust myself with her if I got in a proper state.

Besides, she didn't know what she wanted to let herself in for. She deserved better.

They *did* know—at least partway.

"Chad." Dion was at the side of my bed now. He stood right next to Wynn, who refused to budge for him.

I didn't know if he was being protective or territorial or what. Maybe he just didn't like Dion.

Why couldn't Dion just say whatever it was he had to say? "Dad didn't give you any trouble, then?" I settled my gaze on the strap of my bag over one of Dion's broad shoulders.

Maybe that was why the news hit me so bad.

Maybe if I'd watched his face, I would've seen it coming.

But I didn't, so his next sentence hit me like a train to the gut.

"Your dad's dead." It was delivered quick and concise, like ripping a plaster off. I think I rather preferred it that way, as opposed to having it told haltingly.

Still, it didn't make the impact less jarring. "D-dead?"

How's that possible?

Dion reached out to take my hand.

I saw blurredly Wynn take a step back, body turning back towards me. I couldn't see his expression though, as my gaze was trained on Dion's big, tanned hand clenching around my own pale and freckled one.

"How can he be dead?"

He'd been alive and vicious only a few days ago. I didn't know how many days ago. One? Two? The days were kind of a blur. I didn't even really know what time or what day it was now.

Jeremy stood at the edge of my bed, his fingers tapping against it. He stared at the floor, all silent.

And into the room walked Harriet, her soft smile fading once the tense atmosphere washed over her.

I drew in a deep breath. Better deliver it to her as I'd had it delivered. "Dad's dead."

Her eyes widened in shock then crinkled together in a frown. The expression on her face was impossible for me to read.

It wasn't sorrowful, that was for sure.

There was no love lost between my dad and Harriet. Ever since mum died, Dad hadn't wanted to have anything to do with her.

I didn't want to think about it, to try to decipher whatever it was she was feeling. I tilted my head on the pillow and gazed up at Wynn, who was as stoic as ever.

He stared back down at me, eyes dark and unreadable.

I wished we'd been alone in the room. I needed drugs. Something to make me feel good, to make me forget everything for a while. The drugs the hospital staff had given me weren't doing a good enough job of it. I needed something stronger.

Drugs or alcohol—I wasn't picky.

Just *something*.

My hands were sweating—though I didn't know why, they hadn't minutes before—and the picture I still had pressed to my chest slipped down my side. I made a mad grab for it, managed to twist my upper body enough to hurt my already bruised ribs, and I curled up with a groan of pain without managing to snatch the picture back.

Someone took it from my side.

It had slipped onto the other side of where Wynn and Dion were standing, and when I managed to glance up—eyes hazed from pain—I was met by Jeremy's frowning face as he realised exactly what picture it was.

I bowed my head back down when he looked at me. I didn't want to see what he thought about me nicking a picture of him and Dion on it.

"Chad." Harriet was at the end of my bed now,

and one shaking hand reached down to touch my ankles. "I'm so sorry."

Sorry? For what?

The confusion was only temporary—the reason why she was apologising quickly sank in.

Dad dead.

Me in hospital, beaten up by him and having given myself alcohol poisoning.

"When can I get out of here?" I didn't want to stay in hospital. Too much time on my own, too much time to lie still and think. I didn't like to think. "I want to get out."

"Soon." Dion squeezed my hand, which he'd held onto even as I'd curled in on myself in pain.

That wasn't an answer.

Soon could be everything from the next fucking minute to days ahead. Surely they couldn't keep me for days? They must be getting a lot of young people drinking too much in the A&E? Besides pumping our stomach and making sure we really were all right, what else could they want to keep us for? Surely they'd want to keep the beds clear?

"I don't want to stay here." Everything was better than the hospital.

"Chad? Are you sure you don't want to come with me?" Harriet touched my ankle again, rubbing lightly. "Please. Come home with me."

I shook my head furiously. "I can't."

"Why not?" She didn't understand. That was loud and clear from the confusion in her voice.

But then how could she?

She had no idea what it was like being me, what I struggled with. Losing my bloody mind. I couldn't put her through it, not when she lived alone. If I did something to her… I wouldn't ever be able to forgive myself. She was so *good*. She'd always tried to keep in contact with me after Mum died, even if Dad hadn't liked it.

It wasn't her fault I'd kept pushing her away all these years.

"I can't!" It came out a lot more forceful than I'd intended. Everyone seemed to startle from it, except Wynn, who stood stock still with his arms crossed over his chest. He had a far-away look about him.

While I watched him, he seemed to mentally shake himself, and then he took a step towards the door. "I have to go."

"What—no!" I didn't want him to go. I wanted everyone else to go and him to stay, so he could give me something. Something to take the edge off. "Wynn, no, please."

He stared down at me again, eyes still dark and unreadable. "I'll see you later."

"Wynn!" But there was no point. His back disappeared out the door and I could faintly hear his steps down the corridor. That left me alone in a room with three people who didn't have the faintest idea what it was like to be me. "Make him come back."

"He's gone, Chad." Harriet had brushed by Jeremy, and she now picked up my free hand in hers. Her palms were warm and dry and comforting, but it didn't help at all for the loss I felt at Wynn's sudden absence. "Maybe it's for the best."

"Don't say that." I would've shouted it, but all the fight had gone out of me, I didn't have the energy for it. I didn't have the energy for anything, come to that. I couldn't even move back into a stretched out position on the bed. "Don't say that."

"You'll be out of here soon." That was Dion. At the other side of the bed. His voice reverberated through me, and I closed my eyes. At least he was here. He knew me better than the other two in the room. "You'll come back home with us."

Yes, please.

They weren't throwing me out. Or refusing to let me inside in the first place. That was comforting. Relaxing, even, as I must've dosed right off to sleep after that.

I couldn't remember anything else, anyway.

CHAPTER 16

*J*ust barely made it to the toilet in time.

My knees hit the tiled floor hard, but I didn't even feel it right then as I threw the toilet seat up and bent over as my stomach emptied itself. The little food I'd managed to get down while still in hospital quickly came up again.

I continued to retch even after my stomach was empty, even when there was nothing left to throw up.

It hurt my already sore throat and the spasms going through my body hurt the rest of me.

A panicked sense of déjà vu overcame me as I became short of breathe while still retching.

No, no, not again!

Oh my God, I can't brea—

Someone hit my back several times, which seemed to help.

I slumped forward and rested my chin on the edge of the toilet. I was breathing heavily and everything *ached*.

The toilet flushed and then I was gently pulled back to rest against a broad, warm chest.

My breathing was laboured, but I was slowly calming down as I listened to the calm heartbeat my ear was pressed up against.

My head felt worse than earlier in the day. My hands shook and I was sweating. All of it had started before the nausea. I'd been in bed for hours, but unable to sleep.

A damp washcloth was pressed to my forehead then to both my cheeks and chin.

I blinked my eyes open—they'd fallen shut somewhere along recent events—to see Jeremy crouched next to me. That meant I was currently pressed up against Dion's chest.

That they were Dion's arms around me.

"I-I'm sorry," I managed to get out in a raspy voice.

"Shhh, you've got nothing to be sorry for." Dion whispered it against the top of my head. "I've got you."

I watched as Jeremy walked out of the toilet, only to come back a minute later with a freshly rinsed, cool washcloth that he once again used to wash my face.

A sigh left me as I let my eyes fall closed again.

"You should go back to bed, Jem." Dion was speaking over my head, the deep rumble of his voice reverberating through me. "You have to be up in a few hours. I'll sit with him. I'll call in sick tomorrow morning. They'll have to call in a supply teacher to cover for me, but I can't leave him here alone."

"You sure?" Jeremy still had the washcloth pressed to my forehead and it felt simply wonderful.

Dion nodded against the top of my head. "Yeah. It's Monday. Nothing special going on at college on a Monday."

"Let me help you move him to the sofa, at least. You can't sit on the toilet floor all night."

I pried my eyes open as I was all but lifted up from said floor. I stumbled, but both Dion's strong arms and Jeremy's supporting ones were there to catch me. I was gently put down on the sofa, which was both wide and soft to lie on.

The trip itself from the toilet to the sofa was a blur though. Just as my release from hospital and journey here had been.

It should probably worry me how I couldn't remember much of it—but it didn't. It didn't matter.

I looked up at the two of them now.

Jeremy was biting at his lower lip, looking worried. "Are you sure this is okay? Shouldn't he go back to the hospital?"

"If the withdrawal symptoms from the alcohol worsen, I'll take him to A&E. As long as they're mild he'll be okay."

Withdrawal symptoms?

Dion put his hand on Jeremy's shoulder and squeezed.

I don't have fucking withdrawal. I'm used to drinking, but I'm not a bloody alcoholic.

"Go back to sleep, Jem. You have an early morning."

Jeremy still seemed worried.

Maybe it wasn't all about my welfare. Maybe he was afraid of Dion spending alone-time with me.

I couldn't blame him, if that were the case. I hadn't cared that Dion had a boyfriend back in college. I'd wanted Dion—and I'd got him, only to have Dion tell me it was all a mistake afterwards. That he loved his boyfriend.

Which he clearly does.

I regretted my actions.

I regretted going after Dion with such vigour. If only I'd let Dion help me, instead of trying to get into bed with him... not that we'd ever got into an actual bed. Our little tryst had happened after college hours, yes, but it happened *in* college. In the teacher's lounge, no less.

Jeremy was a nice bloke. He could've left me out in the hallway, told me to never show my face there again, but instead he'd taken me in and been nothing but kind to me. Even once he'd found out who I was.

I couldn't believe myself; how I'd tried to steal his boyfriend away from him. That, thanks to me, Dion had cheated on such a wonderful man.

"Okay." Jeremy nodded. "It seems you know what you're doing." He smiled slightly.

"I do." Dion smiled back, but his was more solemn. "I've dealt with this before. Several times, in fact, when I was just a boy."

Now I glanced at Dion.

He shared a long look with Jeremy, who seemed to be getting *something* out of what Dion was saying.

I didn't though, I didn't get a thing.

Why had Dion dealt with withdrawal symptoms before?

Had it been with Jeremy? Was Jeremy a drunk? Or before he met him?

When I was just a boy… His family, then.

It didn't have anything to do with me though. I wasn't *addicted* to the bloody alcohol, so I couldn't be experiencing withdrawal.

Jeremy gave another short nod. "Good night." His eyes briefly met mine as he turned.

I stared back, somehow unable not do.

A brief smile flitted across Jeremy's lips, another whispered *good night* directed at me, and then he was gone. The bedroom door clicked shut after him.

Dion turned away from me abruptly, and I stared after his back as he disappeared into the bathroom. Once he was gone from sight, I listened to his footsteps.

When he came back, he sat a bucket on the floor underneath me. "Just in case you're sick again," he explained at my curious look. "Sit up a little."

I pushed myself up. It was hard, my whole body protested, but I did manage it.

Dion slid down on the sofa where my head had previously been, and he put one of the cushions over his lap.

I blinked at him, not understanding, and then he gently drew me back down to rest on said cushion. Which again rested on his *lap*.

"Are you sure this is all right?" My head and

stomach felt a lot better when I was lying down. It was sitting up I couldn't handle.

"No, but…" Dion tangled his hand in my hair. "You're sick. I just want to take care of you. I won't let anything happen to you again."

"You can't say that." He really couldn't. "When I'm well I have to leave, so you can't promise that."

"You don't have to leave." His voice didn't sound at all certain though.

"Of course I do. This is your flat. You share it with your boyfriend. You love each other. I'm not going to try and ruin that again. Once was more than enough." I wasn't worth the trouble. If I was gone, they could fix up their relationship without having me around.

"Chad, you didn't—"

"Yeah, I did." Tears pressed behind my eyes but I refused to let them fall. "I still *am*. I shouldn't have come here." There was no helping it, I started crying for real, and it was *embarrassing*.

I wasn't usually a sap, not really. It was only the last few days had been an entire new level of hell than I was used to.

"I'm glad you did come here." Dion's hand softly carded through my hair. "I'm really glad you did."

I buried my face in the pillow as I started to sob.

What the hell's wrong with me?

"H-how c-can you b-be?"

"Because I care about you. More than I should. I just want to help you and make sure you're well. Right now you're obviously not, and I can't stand to see you in pain." He pulled me up to rest against his chest, which caused my stupid tears to leak even faster.

"I don't k-know why you're so kind to m-me. No one ever really is. People don't c-care about me, they don't see me and if they do I'm usually just a l-l-liability."

"Not to me." He hugged me close.

It was too much.

I couldn't take it.

Not the kindness and hope it gave me.

"Don't say that! Please don't say that to m-me." The sobbing wouldn't stop and my laboured breathing hurt my ribs, but I couldn't seem to stop dragging in deep, shuddering breaths. "All I ever wanted was for someone to love *me*, for who I am. But I'm really nothing so how can that ever happen? I'm just a failure in everything and I wish… I wish that it had been me, and not Madison, who died."

"No!" Dion pushed me away from his chest so he could look down at my face. He used his thumbs to roughly wipe the tears away. "Don't say things like that Chad, especially not to me." He was angry. "I don't know what I'd do if anything happened to you, you hear me?"

The sobbing had subsided a bit, but the tears were still falling. "I d-do. But... you and I, we c-can't happen, can we? Jeremy is so sweet, he deserves you. I don't."

"I don't know why you think so badly of yourself." Dion bent over and rested his cheek against my temple. One of his hands slid around to cup my neck while the other dropped to wrap around my waist. "When you're not being cheeky, or depressed, or getting smashed, you're really bright and sweet."

A snort escaped me. "I'm not bright. I failed *everything* in college. I failed my GCSEs and had to retake that year, and I wanted to be smart and do my A-levels, but I *couldn't* do it. I'm a failure."

"I'm assuming you've got a learning disability, Chad, and if that's true it has nothing to do with how bright or not you are. Because you *are* bright, if you would just use your brains for something other than getting smashed and doing drugs."

"Are you still on about that dyslexia thing?"

"I would like for you to get tested. You can get help for it, you know, and then if you want you could finish college. Maybe you could even go to university, if that's what you really want to do."

"I only want a normal life," I admitted in a low

voice. "I just want to be in love. I want someone to love me. To be dedicated to me. No one is."

"Your aunt loves you."

"I know that, I do, and I love her too, but it's not... I don't want to be a bother to her. She has her own life, her own business, she's just met someone and fallen in love... and that's all I want too."

I'd though Dion could be the one, but that was before I'd met Jeremy. Back when I hadn't given a damn about Dion's boyfriend. He'd been unimportant—all I'd wanted was to get my hands on the young, kind, hot teacher.

I was a selfish person.

Not anymore, though.

I'd met Jeremy now.

I couldn't take Dion from him even if there was a slim chance I was able to, not after knowing him. Jeremy deserved to be with the man he loved, and he loved *Dion*.

The man I loved too.

What a mess.

"How was Dad?" The thought entered my mind like a flash and the question had blurted out before I'd even managed to think about it properly. I regretted it now. "You know, when you found him. How was he?" Except I didn't regret it *that* much. I had to know.

Dad was gone—he'd died alone and bitter in his own home.

Just like Mum.

I'd been in shock when Dion and Jeremy had told me the news. All I'd felt was numb. But now I pictured him, in vivid detail, lying dead somewhere, rotting.

Harriet had insisted she'd deal with everything for me.

I'd been too numb to even protest. I didn't want her involved in the mess that was my life, but she'd seemed determined on the matter, and that'd been that. I hadn't been capable of arguing, I still wasn't. If I never saw my dad again, that would be fine. It wasn't like I'd miss him. I'd miss having a roof over my head when I was eventually thrown out of this flat, but until then… I'd just take what I could get.

"He was lying on the floor, face down," Dion revealed in a low voice. "Might've been there a while."

A horrible thought hit me. "Do you think… maybe it could've happened after he beat me and I was unconscious? Maybe he was dead by the time I woke up and left."

"I don't know, Chad."

I stared up at him. He seemed uncomfortable with the entire subject. "It's a possibility."

"Yes, but… Don't blame yourself. It's not your fault, none of it is."

I was surprised at the fierceness in his voice. "He could've been dead while I was lying there knocked out, or when I ran away. He beat me up then went and *died*." Laughter escaped me—hysterical laughter I couldn't seem to rein in. "Rotting in the living room for days." I could picture it in my mind. Grotesque, horrifying images that wouldn't leave me alone. "I know it wasn't my fault, though, not this."

Dion was silent for a heartbeat. "What do you mean *this*?"

"Because it's my fault Mum died." My throat clogged up at the simple thought. "I found her lying on the kitchen floor. I was only eleven. I didn't know CPR or the emergency number. All I tried to do was wake her up, but she wouldn't. She wouldn't wake up."

The grotesque images of my dad's rotting body left me, to be replaced with my mum's lifeless body on the floor. The slide of my hands and knees through her blood. The blood soaking into her matted hair when I turned her head, and then into her blouse when I tried to shake her awake.

"Oh my God," Dion whispered above me, but it was low, like it came from far away. I couldn't decipher the feelings behind the words though. "Chad, that is… that is *not* your fault. Did your dad blame you for that, is that it? Is that the underlying reason he's been beating you?"

"Maybe." I shrugged, awkward in my current position but I did manage it. "I don't know. I think he was beating on Mum before me. All I know is it's my fault."

"He said that?"

I nodded silently.

Dad had said that too many times to count. Though, honestly, if he'd been beating on Mum as I suspected, he couldn't really love her anyway so what was the point in missing her?

Did he miss his old punching-bag?

I wasn't good enough?

"It's not true, Chad. You're not to blame for your mum. You were a kid. Was she sick?"

"I don't think so." I saw the blood in my mind again, pooling on the floor around her. "I don't know. There was a lot of blood."

"Blood?" He sounded alarmed.

"She slit her wrists." Her auburn hair had been matted with blood, and it had lain so that I hadn't been able to see her face. The blood had covered the floor all around her, as well as soaked into her clothes. I'd slid on it as I tried to wake her, getting it all over me.

The memory was so fresh in my mind, even if it'd been years ago she died.

"God." Dion sighed, and his arms around me tightened. "There was nothing you could've done for her. Look… Jeremy and I, we're going to be here for you. Whatever you need, we'll be here. So will Harriet, if you'd just let her. Do you understand that?"

I nodded mutely.

I didn't want anyone to be there for me though. I'd just mess them all up.

I'd refused Harriet's help, because she deserved better. But I couldn't refuse Dion and Jeremy's, because I wanted to be close to Dion. I wanted to be with him—though I knew it couldn't last for long. He had his relationship with Jeremy he needed to fix and I had to let them be.

"Good," Dion was saying above me, but his voice was far away. His hand carded through my hair, and it felt really nice. It grounded me just a little bit. "Everything will be okay. I promise you, Chad. We'll help you and everything will turn out okay in the end."

Doubtful.

Someone in our scenario would be hurt and it was going to be me. How could it be anyone else?

They were grown men who clearly loved each

other, while I was just a big mess. It wasn't possible. I could hope that his words *would* come true, even though it wasn't very likely.

I didn't remember much after that.

I must've fallen asleep.

When I woke up the next morning, I couldn't even face getting out of bed.

CHAPTER 17

"*I*'m not as good as Jeremy, but I think it's edible."

Dion sat a plate down on the table in front of me. He'd managed to drag me out of bed eventually, but only with the result of me lying unmoving on the sofa.

I didn't know why I was suddenly so exhausted, but I was. It happened sometimes. Usually after my most crazy episodes.

"Hey." A hand rubbed my shoulder. "You need to eat."

"Not hungry." I couldn't face moving, least of all actually having to chew and swallow something. I couldn't even get my gaze to move to see what he'd made for me.

The sofa dipped as Dion sat down next to my curled up feet. "Do you want to talk?"

No, I didn't want to talk. I couldn't face talking either. "Talk about what?"

"Whatever you want. I'm here to listen."

No, no, no.

Still, my vocal cords seemed to work on their own. "You said I had withdrawal symptoms last night. I don't. I'm not an addict."

Heavy silence. "Isn't that what every addict says?" His hand came down on my ankle now and he started rubbing gently. "Just wait, once the drugs and alcohol are properly out of your system, your mood will stabilise as well."

I snorted. He thought my craziness was because I was on drugs? Well, then he had a rude awakening coming, once I soared out of the depression that had taken hold. It always lifted—and I felt wonderful for a short time before I crashed hard again.

"You said you'd experienced people in withdrawal before. What'd you mean?"

His movements on my ankle faltered. "My dad was a drunk. Might still be."

"You don't know?" I found the energy to turn my head so I could look at him. He had a pinched look on his face, which I took to mean this wasn't a subject he was comfortable with, but still... I wanted to know. And at least I was talking, right, which had been his point?

"I haven't spoken to anyone in my family for almost fifteen years. I left home at sixteen and I never looked back."

My dad was a drunk.

"Was he abusive?"

Dion nodded. "He was a right arsehole. When he was home, anyway. He tended to stay out with whatever young bird he could find at the time."

"Who took care of you?" Had his dad left him alone, like I'd always been left alone by my dad except when he needed someone to beat on?

"My mum." His smile was bitter. "My mum was at home, caring for my sister and me."

"You have a sister?"

More bitterness. "She's younger than me. I left her behind too." I could tell he regret that particular part, the guilt on his face and in his voice was obvious.

"Why don't you contact her?" I wished I'd had the courage to leave my dad when I'd been sixteen, maybe then things wouldn't be so messed up.

Or maybe they'd be even more. I didn't have any skills I could use to get a job, after all. I'd probably just have ended up living on the streets. I wasn't sure what would've been worse.

"After so many years?" He scoffed, hand tightening around my ankle. "I certainly wouldn't have appreciated it if it'd been me."

"Maybe she's more forgiving." Would I have been, if I'd had a sibling and they'd left me behind when they'd escaped the personal hell? "Or maybe not." I turned my head away, staring at the blank screen of the television without really seeing it.

The darkness seemed to envelop me again and I just wanted to lie there for forever. I didn't ever want to move.

My thoughts went to Dad and how nice it would've been to be dead. I wouldn't have to feel any more if I'd been dead. No more feelings, no more craziness, no more messing up other people's lives.

"Dad's dead." Something had just occurred to me. "There has to be a funeral? Who's dealing with that?"

"Harriet's making all the arrangement," Dion answered. "She reckons you've been through enough —and I agree. You shouldn't have to do that."

"I don't want to do it." Good riddance on him, to be honest. "You think he's rotting?"

"What?" I could just feel Dion's gaze on me, but I couldn't find the strength to turn my head and make sure.

"Bodies rot, don't they? He must be by now."

"I'm sure there're ways of preserving a dead body

until after the funeral." His hand had stilled on my ankle again, but its weight was still there.

"I wouldn't mind if he was." I could just picture it —his fat, bloated body being eaten up by larvas and whatever other insects that made a good meal out of a human body.

"Chad?"

I wondered if the insects would die from eating from him, considering his diet had pretty much consisted of alcohol for so many years. Was he toxic? Had to be, right, with all that alcohol. Couldn't be good for tiny little insects who were only looking for food.

"Chad? Are you feeling all right?"

"Fine." I wasn't. I was lying and I wasn't sure if he could tell or not. Did I want him to tell? Did I want him to call me out on it? "I want to go to bed. I'm tired." I didn't want to get off the sofa, but I wouldn't get any peace and quiet with him around, and I just needed to be left alone.

"Harriet said she'd be over in a little while."

"I can't. Bed." I pushed myself up, somehow found the energy to move, and stumbled into the guest bedroom.

"What about your food?"

I simply closed the door, as I couldn't face

answering him. I fell onto the bed and curled up, drawing the duvet tight over me.

Life was supposed to be happy.

Why couldn't I stay happy all the time?

Why did I get these damn interludes of utter depression?

I hated it so much. It wasn't fair.

Thanks Dad, for really fucking up my life. I appreciate it. Not.

I really did hope he rot.

In the next second I was all up in tears, because *really*, what kind of awful person was I to say something like that about my own dad?

I wished it on myself more, really.

I stayed in bed for the remainder of the day.

I heard Harriet come and go, yet I didn't move. I heard Jeremy come home from work, but I couldn't face it. Like I couldn't face anything today.

Like I couldn't face my fucking *life*.

BY THE NEXT DAY, the depression seemed to have lifted, though I wasn't feeling particularly happy either. But at least I could get out of bed, so I reckoned I could count myself lucky.

It was early too, which means that both Dion and Jeremy would be home still.

And sure enough, when I ventured out of my room I found them both in the kitchen.

Dion was at the table, reading the paper, while Jeremy was at the counter making what looked like a proper English breakfast.

"Morning."

They both turned at my voice. I guess I must've walked rather stealthily over the floor as it seemed neither of them had heard me. Never knew I was so light on me feet.

"Good morning." They said it at almost the exact time, and they both looked me over as if to check if I was all right.

Of course I was, why wouldn't I be? Life wasn't a massive pile of shit today.

I sat down opposite Dion at the table.

Jeremy turned back to the cooker where he preceded to dish everything equally on three different plates.

My stomach rumbled loudly when he sat the plate in front of me. I hadn't eaten yesterday, and before that... I couldn't remember if I'd eaten anything in the hospital. All I could remember from there was pain.

"You seem better today?" Jeremy dug into his

food, while at the same time casting me a quick glance.

"I feel better." I wasn't under a crushing cloud of darkness, anyhow. I'd take the happiness any day though, over this neutral mood where I didn't really feel anything.

I knew Dad was dead, and so was Madison, and though I felt sadness about the last part it was mostly because I knew how much Wynn must be suffering than any on *my* particular part.

They exchanged glances and I wasn't sure they believed me, but they *should*.

"When's the funeral?" Better show them I could deal with things like a grown-up instead of curling up in bed at every bad thing. I wasn't a complete mental case—at least not all the time. I felt rather normal right now.

"In three days." Dion eyed me warily, as if he wasn't sure I'd break or not. Yesterday I might, but today I wouldn't. Today I didn't even know what to feel about anything, it seemed to be so detached from me. Like it'd all happened to someone else, like I was just a spectator, and not the main character in all the bloody drama.

But I was, wasn't I?

I was sitting here, in their kitchen, messing up their relationship even further. They seemed friendly enough now, but surely they hadn't worked things out? If they had, what was I still doing there?

Then again, there was that saying about not looking a gift horse in the mouth or something or another, so I wasn't going to say anything. Staying with them was good.

I could be close to Dion—with his boyfriend's permission even. What could be better than that?

"Harriet wanted me to ask you if you'd like to have dinner with her the day after the funeral?" Dion folded the paper together and put it away to one side. "She wants you to meet her girlfriend."

I chewed on my lip, a stab of guilt hitting me. "Yeah. I haven't actually properly met her. I've seen her, at the hospital, but not spoken to her. I guess I can't decline that. I hear the girlfriend's got a son too. My age."

"I don't know anything about that, but Angelina seems nice enough."

My eyebrows rose. "You're on first name basis already?"

Dion met my gaze head on, unflinching. "We had some time to bond at the hospital, you know, when we were worrying about you."

Translation—when I was getting my stomach pumped and treated for life-threatening alcohol-poisoning.

When I gained my life back and Madison lost his.

Messed up.

Speaking of which, I wouldn't have said no to a drink, but I didn't think they'd appreciate that need, so I kept shut about it. I'd get one sooner or later anyway.

I started in on my food. My inability to muster up hunger or the will to eat yesterday had vanished, and I now shovelled the food into my mouth as quickly as I could chew and swallow it.

"This is delicious," I told Jeremy through a mouthful of eggs and hash browns. "Really delicious."

He smiled. "Thanks." It seemed a bit tight though.

"What?" I could be perceptive to other people's moods.

When I was normal anyway.

I certainly couldn't when I was hyped up mental or dead depressed. Then, I had more than enough with myself, or whatever voices I heard, or things I saw.

But when my mood was stable, when I was my normal self, I could be quite perceptive. Even if I couldn't pass college to save my life. The only reason I'd managed to pass my GCSEs was because I'd had a couple of the same questions second time around.

"It's just my job."

I blinked at Jeremy for a moment before remembering my original question. "You don't like your job?"

"It's a shit job." He shrugged his shoulders, like there wasn't anything he could do about it. "Early shifts are all about an English breakfast, and the late shifts... well, I don't know. The pay is shit, the hours are shit, the place itself is shit. I've got to find something else."

"You're a proper chef? With proper education and all?"

"Yeah. I've been to culinary school. Finished my degree."

"Is it hard to find a new job, then? When you've got the proper training for it?" I popped a piece of sausage in my mouth. "I mean, I can't find a job that wants me to save my life. Not one I like anyway, but then again, I'm not the brightest out there. The opposite actually."

"Don't be so hard on yourself." This was Dion, and his voice was fierce. "If you'd just get tested for learning disability—"

"I'd get a lot of help and special treatment, yeah, yeah." I waved his words away. Nothing I hadn't heard before, after all. It was something he'd tried to get me to agree to since I started the term.

I'd continued to refuse, because honestly... I didn't need some posh fucker to tell me just how stupid I was.

I knew how useless I was at academics, and nothing anyone did would ever change that.

"I want to go back home."

"What?"

They both froze, Dion with his cutlery still on his plate, Jeremy with a forkful halfway to his mouth.

"I suppose it's mine now?" I glanced between them. "I mean, it's not like I can afford to keep it. Or that I even want to, for that matter, but I want to go back and look at it. There's some stuff I want to get." Stuff I hadn't looked at in quite a while—but now, while I was of a sane mind, I wanted to return to it.

"You want us to come with you?" It was Jeremy offering, which was a bit weird, because he wasn't the one who knew me, who supposedly cared about me.

But then Dion was staring at me intently too, so I suppose he did want to know the answer to that question.

Yes.

More than anything.

"If you want. You don't have to." I was good at keeping my emotions in check when my mind was normal. I could bluff my way out of a lot—like I had in the past, whenever child services reared their heads at me.

I could bluff my way out of anything—I could toughen up for anything.

But having them come with me back to the house… that would actually mean a whole lot more to me than I could ever tell either of them in words. Because going back there scared me, even if I knew Dad wouldn't be around to hurt me anymore.

CHAPTER 18

*T*he house was in bad shape.

It smelled *rotten*, and if I had any sense at all—which mostly I hadn't—I wouldn't have gone back in the first place.

If anyone had any sense, they'd tear the entire house down, but I suppose that was impossible what with there being other houses connected to it on both sides.

I ran up the stairs to my room, fell to my knees on the floor, and rummaged under my bed.

"What is it you need?" Dion asked from behind me. I could hear both his and Jeremy's footsteps follow me inside.

"My sketchbooks."

"Why do you keep them under the bed?" Jeremy's turn to question me.

I snagged the handle of the bag I kept my sketchbooks and pencils in and drew it back out. "So Dad won't ruin them in a fit."

Dion walked into my peripheral vision. "You like to draw?"

"Mhm." I checked inside the bag that everything was there. Three sketchbooks, two of which were full and one that was only half full. As well as my pencilcase, filled to the point of almost bursting.

"You didn't take an A-level in Arts, did you?" Dion frowned. I could tell without even looking at him, but when I did turn my head it was confirmed.

"Drawing is one thing I'm good at. I don't want bloody academics to ruin that for me too." If I'd tried to take Arts, I'd probably just have ended up failing that too, like I failed everything. I couldn't take that chance.

It'd been a while since I'd drawn now though.

A while since I'd even had the want or energy to even think about drawing.

It was nice to have the sketchbooks with me again though. They contained a lot—both drawings from when I was of a sound mind and when I was completely mental.

They'd got all my clothes and my mobile phone,

so there wasn't anything else I wanted to take with me, only the bag I currently held. My room held nothing more to me, nothing of importance.

I walked past them silently and headed downstairs.

They caught up with me in the kitchen.

"Hey." Dion's hand squeezed my shoulder and I instinctually leaned into him.

"That's where I found my mum." I pointed. "She was lying on the floor there, right beneath the open cutlery drawer. She'd taken a big knife from it and cut herself up to the point she fainted, and then bled out."

Staring at the spot, my mind brought back the memories of her lying there in a pool of her own blood. Unmoving.

And me... slipping through the blood to wake her up.

"When Dad came home, he raged at me. I think... he threw me away, right into the kitchen table." I felt a twinge in my side at the sudden emerged memory. That wasn't one I'd dwelled on before. "I don't think anyone washed me up for hours. I was covered in dried blood for a long time."

"Jesus." Dion's hand slid around my shoulder now, drawing me in close to him.

My shoulder blades rested against his chest and I turned my head around to bury it in his neck.

I knew Jeremy was there, that this likely wasn't a good position to be in when Dion's *boyfriend* was right besides us, but in that moment I didn't care. I'd take the comfort I could get.

"Maybe his beatings were punishment for me not being able to save her." Did I prefer to think that or that he simply hated me? I didn't know which was the worst scenario. "Maybe a mix of both. Punishment—and the fact that he just didn't like me. He never has. Had, whatever."

He was dead now.

He'd be buried in just a few days.

I wasn't sure I even wanted to go to the funeral, because really, what could I do there? I didn't want to make my peace with him. He was a hateful bastard who'd never given a shit about me.

So I didn't give a shit about him either.

He'd made my life a living hell. It was his fault I was the way I was. I was a big mess because of him and his bad parenting skills.

"Do you have normal parents?" I finally turned around to face Jeremy. His gaze had been resting on us, but I couldn't read his thoughts about the matter.

"I do. Loving, caring parents who've stayed together all my life." Jeremy clasped his hands behind his back then smiled slightly. "I think my mum would love you. She'd mother you to death."

"Must be nice to have such a mother." My voice was hoarse and I cleared my throat to be rid of it.

The hell was I doing getting emotional?

I'd made my peace with mum's death a long time ago, hadn't I?

"Mum died when I was eleven. I remember her before that, but not much. Besides, at eleven was when I needed her the most."

"Because that's when your dad started beating on you?" Dion still held me close to him, his arm not budging around my shoulders.

"That too, but I was thinking more about growing up. I lost my virginity then."

"When you were eleven?" Jeremy's eyes widened in shocked surprise.

I nodded. "Yeah." Was that so unusual?

"That's... young." Jeremy seemed completely taken aback by my admission. I didn't know about Dion, since I couldn't see his face, but his grip around me tightened just the tiniest bit.

"I guess." I shrugged. "It was with an older man. It was nice."

Now I was afraid Jeremy's eyes would bulge out of their sockets. "*Older* man? How much older?"

"Don't know."

I'd been eleven. Everyone had seemed old at that time.

"Around my mum's age maybe? I don't know. He held the funeral, you know, he was the priest or whatever. No one gave a shit about me then. Dad didn't care and Harriet was…" What had Harriet been doing? I had to think hard. "She was wracked with grief. He brought me back into the church once mum was in the ground and we… well, you know. It was nice. He was very gentle."

I didn't have any bad feelings about my first time experiencing sex. I was being completely truthful in that it had been a nice experience. Not good, perhaps, because he'd been big, but he'd been gentle with me and I'd liked it.

In fact, I hadn't stopped having sex since.

While I'd been in thought, they'd been communicating above my head.

"That's statutory rape," Dion said in a low voice close to my ear. "No wait, it's not even that. You were *eleven*, not even a teenager. That was child molestation."

I tensed up, then wrenched out of his grip and spun around to face him. "Don't say that! It was the only good thing that happened to me after mum died. He was a good man who took care of me on the worst day of my life and made me feel just a little bit better." My hands clenched and unclenched in the sudden anger. "If you care just a little bit about me, you should bloody thank him! Who knows, since no one gave a shit about me, I could've just gone off to die myself and have no one care about it."

They still didn't get it.

I could see it on both their faces.

"Fuck this!"

I clutched my bag close as I strode past them.

"Chad!" They both called after me. I could hear they follow me too, which I definitely couldn't have.

Once I made it out to the stairs I jumped down and started running.

I CAME to a halt outside of Wynn's flat.

I saw the lights on in his living room, so I took the stairs two at a time until I reached his floor. I was breathing heavily by the time I was up there, so much so I had to bend over double.

My ribs ached so much I had to straighten again. It was a long run from my house to Wynn's flat—and I hadn't stopped running once I'd started.

I banged on the door, waited for a second, banged again. No answer, but I knew he was there, so I tried the knob.

It turned and the door opened.

I saw Wynn the minute I stepped in.

He sat on the edge of the sofa, bent over the coffee table.

I shut the door after me and walked closer to him, first then seeing what it was he was actually doing. Dividing up white powder with his credit card in two long strips, one of which he promptly snorted.

"Since when do you sample your own merchandise?"

Wynn might be selling drugs, but he'd always been adamant about not doing them.

He finally gave me the time of day, by glaring at me. "Since the police hauled me in for killing my boyfriend."

That drew me up short and my breath stuttered. "They did *what*?" Because Wynn had given him the poppers? "Then why are you out? Are you out on bail?"

"Nope." He popped the p. "I'm free as a bird." He made a flying kind of motion with his hand.

"What happened?" I sank down next to him, my eyes going to the remaining strip of drugs. "Didn't they have anything on you? Not that it's your fault that he swallowed the poppers in the first place."

"Some kind of report came back. Turns out it

wasn't poppers he'd taken, after all." His voice was neutral, but I wasn't fooled.

I'd known him for years—I knew he was upset. The fact he was taking drugs could attest to that in itself.

"They didn't say what it was, as I'm not family and thus not privy to such information, but it was something a lot stronger than that." He leaned back. "They also found a text on his phone. It was written and addressed to me, and it clearly spelled out that it was suicide."

Suicide.

"Oh my God. Wynn—" I turned halfway so I faced him head-on.

He had his eyes closed, his head resting against the back of the sofa.

I'd known Madison wasn't the sanest person around, and he'd clearly had a strange fascination with death, but going from talking about it to actually doing it…

Everything that had mattered to Madison was Wynn. Why would he leave him?

"Don't start with the pity," Wynn snapped. "You're not here for a fucking pity party. If you are, the door's right over there and happy to shut you out."

"I'm not here for that," I protested. "I swear I'm

not. I just, I needed to get away. Dion and Jeremy…
they don't understand. I told them about when I lost
my virginity and they didn't *understand*."

He gave me a side-long look. "No one fucking
understands that, Chad. It's messed up."

I knew Wynn didn't understand—but he didn't
understand much. He was a cold-hearted bastard
who did what he wanted, when he wanted, to whom
he wanted.

I'd be worried about him completely lacking
empathy, but whenever I went mental or crashed into
soul-sucking depression, he was there for me.

"You're lucky, you know," he said. "You've got
two blokes who care about you. They came to A&E
the minute Harriet rang them. They stayed until they
knew you were going to be fine. They might not
understand your fucked up feelings about that
bloody paedophile, but they care about you. Their
actions… they're the actions of people who *care*."

"I…" I didn't know what to say. Of course I knew
they cared, in some way, or else they wouldn't have
let me stay with them. I just wasn't sure they cared as
much as Wynn seemed to imply.

"Whereas I," he continued, "have lost my
boyfriend. He might've been fucked up, but he was
one of the few good things in my life, you know? My
own *mother* didn't come to check up on me when I

rang her and told her I'd been hauled in by the coppers. Still haven't heard a single word from her. But then there's you... you're good. You're all that's left."

He turned his head the other way, but not before I saw the tears welling up in his eyes. "I'm not even allowed to go to Madison's funeral. That fucking bitch of a mother he has hates me and she says she'll have me forcefully removed if I do show up. She hates me when all I ever did was make Madison's life a little more bearable. That's more than she ever managed. That fucking slag."

I slid closer and reached out to him.

"Don't touch me!" Wynn slapped my hand away.

"Don't be such a bloody wanker!" I managed to hook my hand around his neck and drew him in against me. I was surprised he came willingly, after his initial outburst, but then I felt Wynn's tears dampen my jumper.

Wynn had fallen apart, something I'd never seen him do before, and I hugged him close. Being held had helped me many times, both by Wynn and more recently by Dion, when I'd been at the bottom of that black hole of depression.

Being held by both Dion *and* Jeremy had helped a lot.

"I want him back," Wynn whispered, his voice hoarse and broken. "I want him back!"

"I know." I felt my own tears press at the despair in his voice.

If Wynn—cold-hearted, arrogant, better-than-thou *Wynn*—broke down then I didn't stand a chance. I might not have been close to Madison, but Madison had still been my best mate's boyfriend and I *had* considered him somewhat of a friend.

"You can always visit his grave, Wynn, she can't refuse you that." She really was heartless if she couldn't see how much Wynn had cared about her son.

How could she refuse him to go to his own boyfriend's funeral? That was horrible.

"I don't want to visit his grave. I want him *here*." His tears still trickled, but the sobs had stopped. He stayed pressed up against me though, with his face buried against my neck. "I love him. So much."

"I know." I wanted to do something for him, something more than simply hug him close.

I didn't dare stroke his hair or something else to soothe him, however, because I was shocked Wynn even allowed this kind of closeness between us.

He wasn't exactly one for bodily contact. Not unless it was sex or Madison, and Madison... Madison was gone.

"Can you stay here tonight?" Wynn asked brokenly. "Please, just… stay."

I nodded quickly. "Of course I will. You know that. I won't leave you like this." I wouldn't leave him when he was a cried-out mess; he'd never do that to me—though he would've bitched about it— and I would never do it to him.

Neither would he leave me when I was drugged, and now it was my turn.

He was likely cried out *because* of the drugs, as I doubted he'd let his walls down as easily if he'd been sober.

I would stay for as long as he needed me to.

Dion and Jeremy had been there for me, but they didn't *understand*, and I didn't want to go back just yet. I needed to stay away unless I said something I'd regret, and I needed them to get over whatever shock and repulsion they'd felt at my confession.

I would stay here with Wynn.

He needed me.

Because he didn't have anyone either.

"You want the last strip?" He asked once he pulled back from me. He kept his head bowed so I couldn't see his face. "I don't think I should take anymore right now."

I'd forgotten about the line of white powder on

the table, but now my attention was drawn back to it, it called to me.

"Yes, please."

I knew it was stupid. I knew what it would lead to.

But then again, what was wrong about feeling happy?

Nothing at all, that's what, so that's why I almost threw myself over that fine, white line.

CHAPTER 19

I was soaring.

Soaring *so* high.

"Where've you been?" Jeremy strode out of the kitchen, eyes dark and lips pressed together.

I let go off the door, letting it slide shut behind me on its own. I smiled widely at him. I didn't know why, but seeing him felt good. "I've been with Wynn. You know he was hauled off for questioning? They think he *killed* Madison." I snorted. "As if."

Jeremy crossed his arms over his chest, gaze taking me in from top to toe.

"Like what you see?"

His eyes narrowed at my light quip.

Oh well.

"You didn't think to ring or text? We've been

worried about you. We had no idea where you went off to."

"Why are you worried? You don't have to be worried. I'm *fine*. *So* fine." I was fine, the world was fine, *Jeremy* was fine. Dion was fine too, but he didn't seem to be around. "Where's Dion?"

"At work." Jeremy's eyes narrowed further.

I swear, he was too serious. He should lighten up.

"Work?" I scratched the back of my neck, thinking. I'd left them at dad's house on Tuesday and gone to Wynn. Had I stayed with him all Wednesday as well?

"Yes. Work." Jeremy took several steps towards me. "You have any idea how worried he's been?"

"I'm telling you, you don't *have* to be worried. I've never been better!" I threw my arms up over my head and made a little twirl right there on the floor. When I stopped to look at Jeremy again, his frown had deepened. "You know, your face might set like that, and that wouldn't be very attractive, would it?"

"What is *wrong* with you?" He exclaimed. Then he reeled himself in as the entire outbreak seemed to shock him. "Your dad's dead. Your friend's dead. Your dad's funeral is *tomorrow*. How can you be so *happy*?" This was delivered in a calmer tone.

"How can I *not* be?" I countered. "Years of his shit

are behind me. I don't have to deal with him anymore. I'm free!"

"He was still your dad—"

"Sack of shit's what he was." Sack of shrivelled up corpse drenched in alcohol more likely. Now that made a funny picture.

I burst out laughing. "Want to go out with me?"

Another frown. His face really was going to set like that. "Out? Where?"

"Just out. Away from inside into the outside. I mean, who wants to stay inside in a stuffy flat when there's such lovely weather outside? People to meet, things to see. We're in the middle of London! We can go anywhere. Let's go to Hyde Park. I love Hyde Park."

His worried expression didn't lift at all, but he hesitantly agreed. "All right, then." He grabbed his jacket, and as I was already wearing mine, I led the way outside.

The sun shone down on me as I stepped out onto the kerb and I turned my head up to catch the precious light.

"It's so beautiful isn't it? Sunlight. So hot and warm and you get tan! Well, not me, I only get more freckles, but most people get tan. I bet you get tan." I threw him a shrewd look, taking in his tall, lanky body.

He wasn't bad-looking *at all*.

He returned the look. "Your aunt rang yesterday. Had to tell her you'd gone AWOL again."

Why was he talking about Harriet?

We were having a moment of shared appreciation.

That topic of conversation did *not* fit.

"Is she ringing me more now because dad's kicked the bucket? He wouldn't allow me to see her before, but now he's not here to voice his rather violent opinion, it's okay?"

"Your aunt cares about you very much."

"I love her. I really do. I mean, she's my aunt, like. But I don't really know her, you know what I mean? I never went to her with stuff, so she doesn't know me either. We're more like acquaintances really. We're lot a lot alike though. She and mum, they could've been twins, if Harriet hadn't been, you know, younger. And I take after my mum, so I'm very much alike Harriet too, and do you think that's why Dad never wanted her around? Because she reminded him of Mum? Or do you think it was just because he didn't want her messing into his habit of beating me? I think that's rather more likely, to be honest. He always was a selfish git."

I had to stop to draw in breath.

Jeremy was looking at me funny.

"Hey, you're not frowning anymore." I turned on

the watts on my smile. "You're *so* good-looking when you're not frowning. I mean, like, *yeesh*. I could do you."

He blinked. "Umm…"

"But that would be weird, wouldn't it? Considering I've already done your boyfriend. Or he's done me. We've done each other. Whatever. Technicalities, really. Do you think it's weird, me being here now when your boyfriend's had his cock up my arse?"

Jeremy blinked again. "Uh…"

"He's got a wonderful cock, hasn't he?" I continued. "I mean, it was only that one time, but it was *wonderful*. I really want to do it again, like, but you might not like it, would you? Are you two even sleeping together now? Because you seem kind of tense around each other. But you shouldn't be, because he's your boyfriend and he chose you, and he's wonderful and you should appreciate that, like, a lot."

"Chad—"

"But you are letting me stay with you, so maybe you wouldn't mind anyhow? Would you really mind, if I banged your boyfriend again? You could join, too. I wouldn't mind. I enjoy a good threeway. You could double-fuck me, that's proper hot, you know. You ever done that?" I turned my head to face him.

He wore an expression I couldn't read.

"If you haven't, you really should. I've done it several times, and I mean, one cock's awesome, but two's even better! Well, three, with my own in the mix. Not that I do the fucking. I've never done that, you know? Have you? Topped, I mean. I enjoy receiving too much to even think about trying topping. I don't think I'd be any good at it. Though again, I can do anything if I set my mind to it."

"Chad!"

"What?" It was my turn to blink at him now.

We were walking slowly down the kerb, and I bounced on the balls of my feet. It was like my body thrummed with energy.

"Do you ever take a breath?" His lips were parted slightly as he stared at me quizzically.

"Obviously. Still alive, me." I jabbed my thumb against my chest. "Have I really been gone an entire day? Did I miss Wednesday?"

"Eh, yeah. Obviously."

I skipped down the street ahead of him. "Wednesday's overrated anyway. Most boring day of the week. People look forward to Wednesday. I don't know why. What's fun with a day in the middle of the week that's exactly alike every other day of the week? Me, I look forward to Mondays, when it all opens again after being closed. Like today! Today everything's open. Today's Monday!"

"Is this your way of grieving?" Jeremy trudged along at a rather slow pace behind me. *Too slow*.

"Who's grieving?" I twirled around, walking backwards so I could look at him. "Are you grieving? Did I mess up your relationship *so* bad? I really didn't mean to. But I really do like him, you know. And I do want him. He's so handsome, isn't he? Those broad shoulders, the short course hair, the stubble—it's literally to die for. And his muscles—" I made grabbing motions with my hands, just to try and emphasise just how much I wanted to grab onto said muscles.

Too bad Dion was at work.

Work sucked.

Jeremy rubbed a hand over his forehead.

"You too, you know. You're handsome too. You really fit together, you and Dion. A good couple. You know what we should do? I just had the *best* idea *ever*!" I even clapped my hands together like a little girl. "We could all be together. Like, not just for one night or for one shag or whatever, but like together for real. That way we could both be with Dion—but each other too, so there wouldn't be any jealousy or whatnot. God, I'm so *clever*." I turned back around the right way, just barely managing not to walk right into an old lady in the process. "Oh, I'm so sorry, love!"

I didn't know what kind of reaction Jeremy had to my idea, but he was silent, so maybe he was considering it?

He certainly should be.

It was a *brilliant* idea.

The solution to all our troubles and problems and woes.

"Oh snap!" I just remembered. "I forgot my sketchbooks at Wynn's! I have to go get them."

"Now?"

"Yes, *now*. Of course, now. When else would I have done it? We're out now, makes perfect sense to do it." I turned in the direction of Wynn's flat, Hyde Park a forgotten part of my mind by then.

"How is he holding up, your friend?" Jeremy jogged up to my side. "Having lost his boyfriend and all?"

"Wynn? You know about Wynn? You've met?"

"Well, yeah." Now he gave me a funny look. "At the A&E? He was there, obviously. And again when we came to tell you about your dad."

"Right." I drew the word out.

How was I supposed to know they'd met and become all chummy when I'd been unconscious? When I'd been having my bloody stomach *pumped*.

Though Jeremy kept up with me now, I still felt

we were walking too slow. My body still thrummed with energy. So much so I wanted to run.

Actually, it was more like I *needed* to run. I bounced up and down on my feet, forth and back, which only served to earn me odd looks from Jeremy and passer-bys instead of releasing some of that energy.

When we reached Wynn's flat, I ran up the stairs before even telling Jeremy where I was going.

Did he know this was even Wynn's flat?

Maybe he thought I was just running up unknown buildings' stairs.

I banged on Wynn's door, too keyed up to do it slowly and calmly.

"What?" Wynn wrenched the door open, his eyes black and glaring. "Damn it. You're back? What the hell's the rush?"

"Sketchbooks." I jumped up and down on the toes of my feet. "I forgot my bag with my sketch-books. I need them."

Wynn's narrowed gaze took me in. "Did you take anything before you left? You're all hyped up."

"Nope." I popped the p. "I'm all drug free."

"Yeah, right." Wynn snorted, but let the subject drop to walk back into his flat to find my missing bag.

I raced in to help him and located it underneath

the sofa. How it had even ended up under there, I had no idea.

"What're you up to now?"

"Jeremy and I are out for a walk. It's wonderful."

"Jeremy?" Wynn's eyebrows inched up his forehead. "You're spending quality time with your teacher-slash-lover's boyfriend? How's that working out for you?"

"Wonderful!" I threw my arm up in a wave. "*Ta!*" And with that, I thundered back down the stairs.

Jeremy waited at the kerb, hands buried in his jeans-pockets. His jeans fit him rather nicely, showcasing his bum to perfection.

Mmm mm mm.

Why yes, he looked good enough to *devour*.

"Got it!" I waved the bag in front of his face. His rather handsome face. "How old are you?"

He let out a breath. "Twenty-seven."

"Wow. Two years younger than Dion! At least you're not ten years older than me, though. That would be weird, wouldn't it? Like I was only interested in older blokes. Mind you, I *am*, but what would people say about you? Both of you going for a much younger bloke!" I skipped ahead, back towards his flat again.

Life was grand, life was wonderful.

I had my sketchbooks with me, Jeremy following

behind me—and Dion would be home from work whenever college let out.

Whatever time it was now, I hadn't even checked.

I looked forward to spending time with both of my blokes.

CHAPTER 20

*T*oo energetic to sleep, I spent the night on my bedroom floor with my sketchbooks open around me, as well as my pencils spread out between them. My thoughts jumped from one thing to another, which my sketches could attest to, because not a single one was completed.

"Chad?" Dion knocked tentatively on my door.

Draw, draw, draw.

The door protested at being opened.

"Chad?"

Steps on the floor.

"What're you doing?"

A shadow landed over my sketchbook, but I could still see. The pencil flew over the page, and

243

then something else popped into mind and I flipped the paper over to start on something new.

"Chad, the funeral's in only a couple of hours." Dion's big hand came down on my shoulder. "Come get something to eat before we leave. Jeremy's cooking."

"Can't." I turned away from him, bending further over the book. "Busy."

He stayed behind me for a while, I didn't know how long, then he took several steps away.

"Dion, this isn't normal," I heard Jeremy say in a low voice. Probably from the doorway. Sounded like it. "Yesterday he was all happy. He was talking his mouth off, and I couldn't get a word in edgewise. Today he's like this... He needs help."

"He's not a danger to himself. We can't make him."

Danger?

To myself?

Me?

Hah!

Didn't they understand how good I felt?

Didn't they get that I simply *had* to do all these drawings *right* now?

It was important. I couldn't speak and draw at the same time.

"Then what can we do? This isn't right."

"I don't know."

"Stop talking about me!" I snapped. "I'm right here. I can hear you. Nothing's wrong. I'm *good*. You have no idea how good I feel."

"Please come eat." It was Jeremy appealing to me this time. "It's going to be a long day. You'll feel better facing it on a full stomach."

"Not hungry."

"You haven't eaten since yesterday." Dion this time.

"Still not hungry."

"How long've you been up? How long've you been here drawing?" Jeremy.

"Hours." They were messing up my concentration. "*Hours*. Leave me alone."

They did.

Until it was time to leave for the funeral, and then they wouldn't budge.

I grudgingly left my sketchbooks on the floor and went with them, but I wasn't happy about it.

What would I need to go to a bloody funeral for anyway?

It wasn't like he'd been a proper dad.

I didn't want to sit there and listen to some religious fucker's spout of grandiose lies about him.

"Chad." Harriet hugged me tightly once we met

in front of the church. "How are you doing? Feeling?"

I fidgeted out of her hug. "Good. I'm good." I would be good if the prospect of sitting down in a bloody church to listen to prayer didn't make my skin crawl anyway.

"Come on." Dion's hand at the small of my back pushed me gently towards the stairs.

"You're sitting with me right?" I turned to him, suddenly deathly afraid he wouldn't—that *they* wouldn't.

"Of course." Dion reassured me with a small smile. "We and Harriet and Angelina will be in the front row."

Front row.

God.

Not only would I have to listen to some droning old man, but I would have to sit closest to him too.

I could think of a thousand other things I'd rather do.

I'd rather go back to *college* than sit there and listen—and that said a lot, didn't it?

I ended up sitting closest to the aisle, which served me well. If it got to be too much, at least I could just take off without having to shove someone out of my way.

Dad's coffin was up there. Closed, thankfully, because I didn't want to see his ugly mug.

Not that the priest was anything to look at either, old and wrinkly and grey.

Nothing at all like the man who'd held Mum's funeral. He'd been handsome, kind, and caring.

Too bad I'd never seen him again after that day.

Something prickled at the back of my neck while the priest droned on.

I turned my head and found a group of Dad's mates sitting further back. One of them in particular was ogling me. It was the one who'd been doing it before.

"He's watching you. He's always watching."

He was the one who'd rubbed his crotch right in front of me. The old, fat, pathetic creep.

"You're not that desperate. Or are you? Are you so desperate you'd do him?"

I wasn't.

I wasn't.

I wasn't.

I would never let myself in with any of Dad's mates. They were just as low-life scum as he was. Not worth a single thing.

"You should tell him what you feel. What if he does that kind of things to others, hmm?"

Rage flamed up inside me, hot and heavy and all-consuming.

Before I even knew what I was doing I was out of my seat and striding over to him. "Stop looking at me, you dirty old *fucker*. I'm not here for you to lust over. Go home to your fucking wife!"

"That's the way to do it."

"Look at his face."

"He's doesn't like being called out on his perversions."

The man stood up, looming over me as most men did.

It didn't matter.

I could take him.

I could take anyone.

"You show him who's boss."

"Like this do you? Hm? Want a piece of me? You won't be the first. But you know what? You're disgusting and I never want to see your fucking face again."

"Yes, that's the way to do it!"

Arms locked around my waist, dragging me back.

"No!" I trashed against them. "Let me go! He's a fucking pervert. He's got no right to look at me. Let me GO!"

I was dragged out of the church by those strong arms. I thrashed and kicked and screamed then fell sobbing to the gravel once I was let go. It dug into my knees and hands, but I didn't care, I just curled in on myself.

"Chad." Dion's voice, all low and soothing. "Has he hurt you? That man, has he done anything to you?"

"He wants to," I sniffled. "He wants to hurt me."

"Has he told you that?" Jeremy this time, on my other side.

"It's obvious. He keeps staring at me. Whenever he's over at Dad's, he stares at me like I'm something to be devoured. He rubs himself, like he can't wait to get his fucking dick in me one way or another."

Someone drew a deep breath.

I was pretty sure it was Harriet.

"Everyone's just using me, like I'm expendable. I'm not worth anything to anyone." My sobs came quicker now, the tears rolling from eyes that burned. "Why doesn't anybody like me? I just want someone to like me."

"Hey, *shh*. Come here." Dion drew me up and in against him, and I buried my face against his chest, taking all the comfort I could.

"Harriet, he needs therapy." This was someone else. Another woman. Must be Harriet's girlfriend.

Had everyone followed me outside?

Did everyone have a bloody opinion on my psyche?

Just like that, I was fuming with rage again. "Don't talk about me like I'm not here!" I pushed out from Dion to glare up at them, and true enough, the one who'd spoken was Harriet's blonde girlfriend. "I *am* right here and I can hear you and you have *no* right whatsoever to make any sort of decisions for me!"

"That's not what she meant." Harriet held her hands up, palm out. "But Chad, you've been through so much lately. For a long time, even, if what Wynn said was true. Two people close to you have died and you're clearly depressed. You *need* to talk to someone."

"I don't need shit," I snarled. "I need for everyone to leave me the *fuck* alone!"

"Chad, your mum—"

"Don't mention my *mum*!"

"But you need to—" Harriet was close to crying, I could tell.

Good.

As long as she left me alone, I would leave her alone. But as long as she was on me, she'd get the same in return.

"It's my life! No one else gets to make decisions!"

"Chad, don't you remember?" Harriet was pleading with me now. Pleading for what, I didn't know. I didn't *care.*

I started laughing. "Remember? Remember what? Every time Dad beat up on me? Because I got to tell you, I've lost count. Remember him beating on Mum? Yeah, I think I do. I understand why she couldn't take anymore. I can't take anymore either, not more crap!" I burst out in another fit of laughter.

"Is he high?" Jeremy muttered behind me. "Has he been using drugs in our flat?"

I whirled around. "Maybe I *have*." I hadn't. "I can leave if it bothers you."

"Where are you going to go?" Jeremy stared at me hard. "You don't want to go with your aunt. Are you going to live on the streets?"

"I could, if I wanted to," I said, defiant. "Why do you care anyway? If I leave, you'll have your boyfriend all to yourself. Wouldn't that be nice?" The venom was thick in my voice.

"Chad, please!" Harriet's shrill voice brought me back around to face her, Jeremy forgotten about again. "You have to talk to someone. Your mum—"

"I told you *not* to mention my mum!"

"My baby boy. You've grown so big."

I pressed my hands to my head and squeezed my eyes closed. "Shut up, shut up, shut up."

"No one's speaking, Chad." Hands were on my shoulders, squeezing tight.

Everyone was speaking.

The voices were trying to talk over each other and it was all just a jumbled mess I couldn't make anything worthwhile out of.

"Take me home," I pleaded. "I want to go home."

Dion hugged me close, his strong arms wrapping tight around me. "Don't you want to go back in? The funeral's just started."

I shook my head ferociously. "No. Take me away from here. I don't want to be here. I want to go home."

"All right, all right. We'll go home."

"Chad…" Another hand pressed against my back. From the voice I knew it was Harriet, but I couldn't face turning to look at her. Being pressed up against Dion's chest was more than enough at the moment.

At least the voices had quieted down.

"I have to stay here until the funeral's over."

"You wanted to meet for dinner tomorrow?" It came out muffled, as my face was buried in Dion's shirt.

"If you're up for it, I would appreciate that very much. I'm finished at the Café at five, why don't you come down and meet me there?" Her palm ran over my upper back in a caress, and she seemed to hesitate pulling her hand away.

"Okay. That sounds good."

"I hope you'll feel better by then. If you don't, just ring me and we can reschedule. I'll understand."

"Yeah. Okay."

Dion, with one arm resting over my shoulders, turned me around and started leading me away from the church.

"I swear to God, I've never looked at the lad," someone insisted further back, but I was too exhausted to confront the perverted bastard again.

I'd said my piece.

He knew I was on to him.

And it wasn't like I'd ever be in the same vicinity as him again.

I was pressed up against Dion on one side, and Jeremy walked close on the other. They didn't have a car—didn't need to in the middle of London—so we'd taken the bus.

We walked to the bus stop in silence and sat down to wait.

I leaned forward and buried my face in my hands, too embarrassed to look at either of them. "I'm sorry I ruined the funeral. I mean, not because I owe it to him or anything, but because of how I did it. I just couldn't sit there and let him leer at me any longer."

"You sure he was looking at you?" Dion hedged. "There were more rows of people behind you, you know."

TT KOVE

"Of course it was me. He's always looking at me whenever he's around. Last time I saw him he rubbed his bloody crotch right in front of me."

"Right, I see." Dion rubbed my back in big, soothing circles. "What did your dad have to say about that? Didn't he mind?"

"I don't think he ever saw. None of them did. Dad's mates, I mean. They're not exactly supporters of gay people, Dad and his mates, so I'm pretty sure it only happen when none of them saw anything."

"You sure it was meant to you, Chad?" Jeremy asked quietly.

"You don't believe me?" My mood was sinking. The day had started out so good, so *focused*, and now I was heading to the gutter again.

I'd thought the happiness would've lasted longer than this.

It usually did.

"I believe you believe it," he said diplomatically. "But misunderstandings can happen."

Misunderstanding indeed.

What did he know anyway?

y energy levels started rising again Friday evening, and after a couple hours of sleep, I was too keyed up to stay in bed anymore. I tried to move around the flat silently, doing some drawing, watching some telly, but my thoughts kept jumping around and nothing could hold my attention.

I got horny, so I wanked off in the bathroom, but it wasn't enough. My body needed more than my own hand.

When Dion emerged to head to work, I was all but vibrating with lust.

"You awake already?" He smiled at me as he passed me to head into the bathroom.

"Couldn't sleep. But it's all good."

"You feeling better today?" He took me in from top to bottom.

Better?

I felt *fantastic*.

Except for the small fact that I desperately needed to get laid.

"Absolutely."

He nodded once then opened the bathroom door. "Sorry, I can't chat anymore, I'm late for work. I have to hurry to get in on time."

I sat twiddling my thumbs waiting for him to come back out, but once he did he instantly headed off to get his outerwear on.

"I'll see you tonight, okay? Don't forget your dinner with Harriet."

"I won't." I waved him off then looked around desperately for something else to do.

Dion might've headed out, but there was still another handsome bloke in the flat.

I wondered if he was awake or if Dion had managed to sneak out without disturbing him.

Had they had sex last night?

Had they had sex at all since Dion'd had sex with me?

I inched over to the bedroom door. Dion hadn't closed it properly so all I had to do was push and it swung open.

There was a lump on one side where Jeremy was buried under the duvet, while the other was clearly left in a hurry.

I walked slowly over to the empty side.

Jeremy's chest rose and fell slowly, so he was clearly still asleep.

"Jeremy?" I put my knee up on the bed. The mattress dipped under my weight. "Jeremy?" I raised my voice.

"Mmm?" Jeremy rolled over onto his back. He struggled with opening his eyes, but they finally did open.

I put my other knee on the bed as well.

"What's wrong?" He blinked blearily at me.

"Nothing." I put my hands down so I could properly crawl atop the bed. "Nothing at all's wrong."

He rubbed his hands over his face, ran one through his hair, and then pushed himself up on his elbows. "Dion left for work?"

"A while ago." I was properly on the bed now.

He eyed me sideways. "You sure everything's all right?"

I nodded slowly, unable to tear my gaze from him. My body thrummed with the lust coursing through me. "If you don't count my little problem, anyway."

"Little problem?" He seemed utterly baffled.

Maybe because he'd just woken up?

Surely that had been a blatant innuendo.

I cast my gaze downwards.

He followed my line of sight, understanding dawning on his stubbled face.

I lifted my head slowly, gaze on him again.

No time to waste.

I moved quick, over to his side of the bed, and straddled his hips. I didn't give him any time to do or say something before I kissed him.

His elbows gave way under him, so we both fell back down on the bed, but I kept on kissing him.

He was unresponsive so far, which definitely wouldn't do.

"Chad." His hands pushed against my shoulders. "Chad. What're you doing?"

"Let it go, Jer." I, in turn, cupped his face in my hands. "Just feel."

"Dion's my boyfriend," he protested, but he didn't push me away any further either. "And he cheated on me with you."

"Then you can cheat on him with me, too. Even the playing field." I rocked my hips down against him. I was hard and ready to go, but the duvet was so thick I couldn't say what state he was in.

Judging from his protests, it wasn't much of a state.

Yet.

"I like you. I really do. I like you both." I rocked down against him again and moaned at the pressure against my cock.

"Chad…" He sounded more uncertain now. *Seemed* more uncertain too.

His hands keeping me at an arms' length faltered, and I dove back in for another kiss. This time I even added some tongue. Nothing got blokes going faster than a slip of the tongue.

"You can do anything you want to me," I whispered, lips against his. "Anything you want. Except topping. I don't top."

"Chad, we shouldn't…" But his grip, which had moved from pushing at my shoulder to grip my upper arms, tightened.

I kicked the duvet down his feet then finally managed to grind my hard cock down against him properly. He was only sleeping in his boxers and his half-hard dick told me clearly he wasn't exactly uninterested.

"Fuck," Jeremy groaned, his head tilting back a bit.

"That's right." I grinned wide. "*Fuck.*" I slipped my hand down his boxers, and again earned a muttered *fuck* in return. He was only half-hard, but I'd get that taken care of in a blink. "You want me bad, don't you? I know you do. Have known it since we met."

I got my own dick out and our hips rolled together in sync, rubbing our private parts together all deliciously. I aligned our cocks and stroked us both at the same time, which had an immense effect as Jeremy hardened right up.

"Yeah, *yes*," I hissed, bucking my hips in time with my strokes.

"Bloody hell." Jeremy was flushed under me. He looked good like that, with eyes shrouded by pleasure.

I bent my head down to nip at his neck, pleased when it earned me a moan. "Sex is so great. Don't you just love it? Don't I make you feel *so* good?"

His breath stuttered in his throat. Our cocks were leaking pre-come all over each other.

"I'm not going to last," I whispered next to his ear before nipping at the lobe.

My free hand tangled in Jeremy's hair, pulling slightly on it as pleasure racked through me—not enough to hurt but enough to be felt. There was nothing quite like having another cock in the mix, whether it was rubbing against my own or in my arse.

"M-me neither," Jeremy gasped out.

I stroked us both off confidently. "You feel so

good against me." I turned my head to nip on his lower lip now.

It didn't take Jeremy long at all to reach climax. He shot over my hand and my jumper, as well as his own tee.

I wanked myself off furiously so I could join him in the post-coital bliss, and I messed up his tee even further when I shot long lines of semen over it.

Once I was dry, I collapsed atop Jeremy, who was busy getting his own breath under control.

"Well. This was a monumentally bad idea."

My whole body went from happy and limp to angry and pulled tight. "How so? This was an *excellent* idea." I pushed myself up. I was still straddling him and both our bare, limp cocks rested against each other's.

"*How* was this a bad idea?" He stared at me as if I was mad. "How about me cheating on my boyfriend? With the bloke *he* cheated on me with in the first place?"

"You *liked* it." I jabbed a finger in the middle of his chest. "Your spunk's all over me, which is evidence enough." I clambered off him to stand on the floor. "I did something nice for you and you don't appreciate it."

"Wha—" He pushed himself up. "You did something *nice* for me? What am I, your fucking charity case?"

If looks could kill, now would be the time to access that particular skill. "No, I'm yours, aren't I? Your charity case. Take care of the poor lad who can't take care of himself. Who's beaten by his dad, who doesn't want to stay with his aunt, who took your boyfriend from you, and who's now ruining your life."

"I never said you were ruining—"

"I know what I do," I snapped. "I might be mental, but I know that much." With that, I turned on my heel and stormed out of there.

Stormed out of the flat, in fact.

I was lucid enough to grab my shoes on my way and my jacket, but that was it.

It was early morning still, and I spent hours wandering around trying to be rid of the restless energy.

But it didn't go away.

If anything, it rose in intensity.

It felt like I was crawling all over and the need for sex returned full force.

I strode into Harriet's Café.

"Where's Harriet?"

There was a black-haired bloke at the counter. I was too busy looking around for red hair to pay attention to him.

"Not here."

"I'll just have to wait then." And I brushed past him to head back to the break room.

When I entered it, it turned out I wasn't alone.

A blond bloke had been sitting on the sofa, but he rose once I opened the door. "You must be Chad." His eyes were green, gaze trained on me.

He wants me.

He wants me bad.

I pushed on his shoulders hard so he slammed back against the wall, and then I crowded in close to him. "You can have me."

"Wha—What are you doing?" His Adam's apple bobbed heavily as he swallowed and his hands fluttered nervously in front of him.

I grabbed both his wrists and forced them to the side, up at shoulder-height.

"P-please." His voice was thin, small.

"Like to beg, do you? That turns you on?" I was game with that. Everything turned me on, after all.

"Please don't hurt me." Wide green eyes stared back at me.

"Hurt you? Oh love, I'm not ever going to hurt you. I'm going to make you feel *so* good. Like you've never felt before."

He was trembling.

From lust, obviously.

Why wouldn't he be, right?

I thrust my hips forward, against his, and his breath hitched.

The door behind us opened, pleasant voices drifting over to me, until they suddenly stopped mid-sentence.

I turned my head around. "Do you mind? We're kind of busy here."

Harriet stared back at me with wide eyes, and behind her was her blonde girlfriend. I couldn't even remember her name.

"Mum," the bloke I was pressed up against whimpered.

I turned back to him with narrowed eyes. We were about to get hot and heavy, so why in the world was he calling for his *mummy*?

"Chad, let go of him." Harriet came closer.

My head whipped back around. "Don't tell me what to do!"

"Let him go!" Harriet's girlfriend stepped around her. Her hand grabbed onto my upper arm and she shoved me away.

I was so surprised I let her, and I stumbled back.

She turned to the bloke, the hand that had grabbed me now going around his shoulder. "What do you think you're doing?" Her eyes bore into me.

"No, what do you think you're doing?" I advanced on her. "And you!" I turned to Harriet. "What do *you* think you're doing? Disrupting us while we were in the middle of something. Stop ruining my life!"

"Chad, I'm not—"

I ran out of there.

Originally I'd planned to leave the café altogether, but I ended up in the kitchen.

A blond bloke was in there, cutting up onions. I ran up behind him, wrenched the knife from his grip and turned it on him.

He jumped back, eyes wide and hands up.

"Get away." I jabbed the knife at him.

"Chad!" Harriet came into the kitchen now, once again followed by her *faithful* girlfriend. "Chad, what are you doing?"

"This is what you want isn't it?" I turned the knife on myself, pressing the blade against the thin skin on my neck. "If I do this, you won't have to deal with me anymore. No one will have to deal with me anymore. My mum did it, so why can't I?" I pressed it in further. The blade pierced skin and I felt blood start to trickle.

"Chad, no!" Harriet was crying.

Her girlfriend had a phone to her ear but voices were speaking above each other again now, so I couldn't pinpoint her exact words out of all of them.

I squeezed my eyes closed. "Shut up, shut up, shut up!"

"Chad?"

"I said *shut up*!"

"Please give me the knife—"

"Shut up!" I backed away.

All the voices…

The knife still pierced my skin, the blood running down my neck into my jumper.

"Do it. That's all you're good for, isn't?"

"Do like your mummy. Be like your mummy."

"Do it, you little piece of shit. I wish it had been you and not your mum."

Sobs escaped me.

Dad was supposed to be dead. He wasn't supposed to be speaking to me. Why was he *here*? He should be six feet deep in the ground now.

A hand closed around mine, trying to take the knife. I jerked back, despair so quickly replaced by rage my head spun.

"Don't touch me! You fucking bitch! Let me go!" I tried to wrench the knife back, but whoever it was had too good a grip on it.

My hands were empty all of a sudden, blood still trickled and I was *raging*.

I pushed whoever was close to me, pushed hard, and I heard the clatter as they slammed into the counter.

Good.

Good for them.

Let them hurt like I hurt.

In the next moment, I was the one who was pinned.

I trashed and flailed, the rage blacking out everything but my violent movements to try and break out of the restraints.

I didn't know how long I fought, but eventually I found myself *actually* restrained on hands and feet—atop a gurney.

"Chad, it's going to be okay," I heard Harriet say from somewhere, but I was still fighting, still raging, and I had no sight for anything but my own struggle.

"Let me go! Letmego, letmego, letmego!" I screamed, using all lung capacity, and they better listen to me, they better, because I was being serious. "I'm going to fucking *kill* you!"

Eventually I think I passed out.

Or was sedated, more likely.

All I knew was that eventually, everything turned black.

PART IV
JEREMY

CHAPTER 22

I was on the sofa, head tilted back, twiddling my thumbs in nervousness, when Dion came home from work.

I jumped up, sat back down, and then stood again.

"What's wrong?" He eyed me weirdly.

"We need to talk."

God, was this how he'd felt when he'd had this talk with me? This feeling sucked.

I didn't want to have the talk at all, but I knew I had to tell him. Most of all because he needed to know, but also for my own conscience and because he'd told me in the first place.

He was wary now, I could tell, but he sank down on the other sofa. "What's wrong?"

271

God, how was I supposed to word myself? "After you left for work this morning…" I wished I didn't have the day off. That way I could've put this off for a few more hours while still at work.

But alas, I had a lot of free time as I didn't exactly have the best job.

Definitely time to look for a new one.

"Is it Chad?" He frowned.

"Well, he's part of it all right."

Deepening frown. "What happened?"

"He woke me up after you left. I don't know the exact time, but I was asleep, so it couldn't have been long after."

"Was something wrong?"

"That's what I thought too. Turned out there wasn't so much anything *wrong* as anything *up*."

"What?" His worried frown turned into one of confusion.

"He was turned on." Better to come out and say it. Part of it, anyway.

"For you?" He leant back now, surprised.

"Is that so hard to imagine?" It came out. I hadn't meant to say it. It wasn't like I could be offended after all, as it was Dion Chad was in love with.

And Dion with him.

"Thing is, I don't think it mattered if it was me or you. If I'd been the one heading out to work, I think he would've been on you. It was like… Like he was possessed or something. I don't know."

"Yeah." Dion went back to frowning. "So… you two? Did—"

I nodded quickly, finally admitting to the whole thing. "I was half-asleep, Dion, and he was on me and it felt *good*. I know it's not an excuse, but it's the only one I have."

Besides, you cheated on me.

But that would be a petty thing to say. Like just because he cheated on me, I was entitled to cheat on him.

He drew in a couple of deep breaths, then ran his hand over his face. "Where is he now?"

"He ran out in anger. I don't know where he is." I licked my lips nervously. "He's supposed to be to dinner with Harriet now though. Maybe he'll be back soon. He's had hours to cool off, after all."

I hadn't before finished speaking when the door-bell rang.

Dion pushed himself up, and with one long look down at me, he went to open it.

"Can I come in?" I heard Harriet's voice coming from the hall, which spurred me into motion.

"Aren't you supposed to be having dinner?" I met them in the hall, where Dion had let her in.

I took her in slowly. She looked dishevelled and

her eyes were red and sore. *She's been crying. Oh God, why has she been crying?*

"We should sit down."

Dion was thinking the worst, I could tell, but dammit, so was I.

We sank down on the bigger sofa now, while she took the smaller one.

"There was never any dinner, we didn't get that far," she started in a low voice. "Has Chad told you about his mum?"

I glanced at Dion.

He sat stiff, but his thoughts were obviously churning.

"He said she killed herself. Slit her wrists."

"Yes, she did. But has he told you why she did it?"

"He never gave a reason, no. But he seemed pretty torn up by it. He was the one who found her." Dion dragged a hand through his hair.

"Kendra was bipolar." Harriet glanced between us. "It's also known as manic-depression. It's a hereditary condition, which she got from our father, and he presumably got from someone else. If someone's bipolar in your family, there's a very high chance that someone's bipolar before you, even if it's never been diagnosed before."

Dion drew in a sharp breath.

I had a feeling where this was heading, but I didn't know how to react. I'd heard the term manic-depression, but I wasn't sure what it was exactly.

"It skipped me, and I'd hoped it had skipped Chad as well. But ever since Kendra died, Bryce didn't allow me to see him and certainly not spend any quality time with him. When he got old enough to decide for himself, he was too busy with other things. So I never saw the signs, because I'm pretty sure they've been there all this time." She buried her face in her hands, sniffling a bit. "I started fearing him having it at the funeral. That wasn't normal behaviour, after all."

"I just figured it was grief," I shot in. "Everyone deals with grief, and the stress it causes, differently."

"If he hadn't had the bipolar genetics, perhaps. But he has it, I know. He hasn't been diagnosed, obviously, but I recognise the behaviour. He came into the Café today, hypersexual and irritable. He accosted my girlfriend's son, who has a past that didn't make that a pleasant experience for him, and then he grabbed a knife, threatened one of my staff with it, before turning it on himself."

"What?" Dion barked out, leaning forward, on high alert.

"He only pierced the skin on his throat. It looked worse than it was because of all the blood. Damian, another employee of mine, managed to take the knife from him eventually, when he was distracted by auditory hallucinations." She swallowed heavily, her eyes filling up with tears. "I've done it before too, with Kendra. She had psychosis as well."

"Psychosis?" Dion seemed to be choking up too.

I had to admit, this did *not* sound good.

"Trademark of bipolar I. Psychosis while manic." Harriet's hands were shaking. "Angelina called 999. They came and restrained him, and brought him to hospital. He's been sectioned. He needs treatment."

"What kind of treatment is there? What can they do for him?"

"It all depends. Medication never worked well for Kendra, but I hope they can for him. He needs medication, and he needs to stay away from alcohol and drugs. He needs a regular sleeping pattern and no stress. Those were things drilled into us from early childhood, about our dad, and then again when Kendra was diagnosed."

Something else occurred to me. "Hypersexual?"

Harriet nodded. "Another trait of mania."

Maybe that was the explanation then? Why he'd come onto me. Maybe he didn't fancy me at all.

I didn't know how to feel about that.

"The symptoms have been there the entire time," Dion was saying next to me. "I just didn't… I didn't think he was actually mentally ill. I just thought… hell, I don't know what I thought."

"If he didn't tell you about his mum then it's not the first conclusion to make. If you know a child has a bipolar parent *then* it's much easier to see the signs for what they are."

"So he's in hospital now?"

"Yeah. They had to sedate him." More tears filled her eyes. I was afraid they'd spill over soon.

"Only family's allowed then?"

"I'm sorry." And she seemed truly sorry. "He's being sectioned whether he wants to be or not. He's a danger to himself and others. I don't know if he's done anything dangerous before, but seeing him with that knife… God. It was horrible. I think Leslie's going to need therapy after. My employee, that is. Not to mention Josh, but then he's already in therapy." She was rambling now.

"Hey." I leaned over to put both my hands on top of her shaking ones. "They're going to help him now. He's going to get the help he needs."

"What kind of aunt am I, though? I never saw it." She kept her head bowed, and her voice was choked.

"You said it yourself, you never saw him. He's been with us for days now, and we didn't even suspect it. Though now I hear about it, it was very obvious."

Harriet nodded fervently. "I should've tried more to see him. To fight Bryce. If I'd known what he'd been doing to Chad…"

"He went out of his way to hide it." I didn't understand why he had, because his aunt clearly loved him and she would've done anything for him, but then Chad hadn't exactly taken the best life choices lately. Or ever. "This isn't your fault."

"Feels like it is." She sniffled again. "I'm his only other family."

"Lots of people saw him a lot more than you did." Dion finally spoke up again. "And no one did anything. Including me. I should've recognised it. I just… I thought he was eccentric. And on drugs."

Harriet raised her head, gaze locking on Dion. "Which he is. He gets them from Wynn. And drugs… They induce the mania. They always did for Kendra. She did them too, and he's just… he's walking in her footsteps." A somewhat hysterical laughter escaped her. "God, I should've seen it."

"Don't beat yourself up over it," I tried to soothe her.

"I, out of everyone, should've recognised the signs. I grew up with my dad, with Kendra…" She sighed and shook her head. "I should go. I just wanted to come here and tell you about the current situation."

Dion jumped up the moment she stood.

I followed more slowly.

"Will you tell us how he's doing? And when we can see him?"

Harriet glanced between us. "You really do care about him. He must about both of you too, since he agreed to go with you when he wouldn't come with me."

I wasn't so sure he cared about me, but he definitely cared about Dion, and it was reciprocated.

And I could kind of see what Dion did see in him. He was oddly charming, though now that I thought about it, some of it might've been because of the mania. Especially that day we'd been out walking and he just wouldn't shut up.

Not to mention this morning…

I don't know what she saw on our faces, but it made her smile a wider smile than I'd seen till now. "I'm sure he wants to see you as soon as possible."

"Do you have any timeframe? For how long it'll take them to diagnose him and allow visitors?"

She shook her head sadly. "He's psychotic. He can't see anyone at the moment. They'll set to medicating him right away, but there's also about finding the *right* medication."

"Right? Are there so many to choose from?" I must've been real sheltered in my childhood, been around exceptionally healthy people. If I *had* known anyone with a mental illness, they'd hid it well.

"Yeah. There's so much to consider. He can't be on antidepressants for when he's depressive, for instance, because they tend to induce mania. It's an advanced puzzle the doctors have to solve. They never quite managed with Kendra, but I hope they can with Chad."

"So do I," Dion whispered. "So do I."

CHAPTER 23

"So what do we do now?"

Harriet had left and we were both on the sofa again. Next to each other this time.

I could feel the warmth from him from our almost-touching shoulders. I longed to just drag him close, but I was afraid I'd ruined it all by being angry with him for weeks and then doing the very same thing I was angry at him for doing.

"I don't know." Dion ran his hands over his face, rubbing against his eyes. "That day I slept with him… I think he was manic then too. Manic, and hypersexual, and hallucinating. He kept saying things, like he was replying to something he thought I'd said. Things that I never did say."

"Like what?"

"Like 'I love you'. I didn't say those words to him, but he told me he loved me *too*, which now leads to the obvious conclusion of auditory hallucinations. He also said something about stars..." He fell into thought. "God, maybe he had visual hallucinations as well."

"I don't think he had any hallucinations this morning. He was just very..." I flailed my hand, searching for the right word. "Sexual."

Dion turned his head to look at me. "We've made a mess of this, haven't we?"

"Of Chad's situation?"

"That too, but I meant our relationship."

"Yeah." It came out on a low breath. "I don't want us to grow apart. I like what we have."

"But?" he prompted, because obviously there was one.

"But you feel something for Chad, and, well, I kind of like him too."

Dion cleared his throat uncomfortably. "So where does that leave us?"

"With a threesome?"

Chad had suggested it right smack in the middle of mania, I knew now, but the words had resonated with me.

I felt sorry for him obviously, but I also felt attracted to him. He was handsome, no doubt about that now the bruises were starting to fade, but he was also a sweetheart to be around.

When he wasn't depressed or completely manic, anyway.

So his words... I'd been mulling over them for days.

"A threesome?" Dion blinked in surprise.

"I don't know." I looked away, not at all certain. "It was something he said, but in light on recent events I realise he was completely manic when he did say it. But he said we could be together all three of us. It got me thinking. I've been mulling over it for *days*. And I mean, why not?"

"That's the kind of thing that only happens in romance." But he did seem thoughtful.

"No, it's not. I mean, obviously there must be people out there who are in love with more than one person? Who are in a relationship with more than one person?"

"Isn't that what they call an open relationship? That's what you want?"

"No!" Of course it wasn't. "I don't want to be with anyone else. Just... I want the three of us to figure things out between us. I don't want other people to be a part of it, just the three of us. Isn't that enough?"

"Yeah, I guess." He drew his lower lip in-between his teeth, worrying it.

"You want him, Dion. You have for a long time. And while you were his teacher, that wasn't a very good idea. Sleeping with him wasn't. Illegal too, probably. But you're not his teacher anymore. You wanted to help him out and you messed it up—but we've both got the chance now, haven't we? I want to help him too, and now we know exactly what's going on, it'll be easier."

"So a relationship between three people?"

I wasn't at all certain it would work out, or if Chad would be interested in it. After all, what might've been a good idea while manic might not be so when he was back to normal.

"Yeah." I turned on my side and scooted closer to Dion, putting my hand on his thigh and squeezing. "I've been angry these past weeks—and I did have a right to be. Until I went and did the very same thing, anyway. But it's the solution you need, isn't it? This way you don't have to feel guilty choosing either one of us. If things don't work out with me and Chad then you and him can still be together? And you and I, at the same time?"

His hand inched out, gripping my shoulder. "You would really be okay with that?"

"I think so." It was my turn to bite down on my lower lip. "I think we can try, at least."

He stared at me for what must've been an entire minute, then drew me in close and kissed me.

It'd been weeks since we'd kissed now, and I melted right into it. I'd missed being close to him, I really had, but my own anger had kept us far apart.

Even when Chad had occupied the bedroom, and we'd *had* to share a bed, we'd both stuck to each our sides.

Those weeks were over.

It was time to reconnect, because there was nothing I wanted more than to be with him. We'd been together two years already, and I wasn't prepared to let him go.

If that meant giving a threesome a chance, or an open relationship where he could be with just me and Chad a chance, then I was willing to take that.

Because I couldn't lose him.

He meant everything to me.

I WENT to the Café the next day to have lunch with Harriet.

Dion was at work, and I had the late shift, so it wasn't possible for the both of us to go together.

Harriet was wiping the counter furiously when I entered, worry-lines etched into her forehead. She was so set on her task she didn't even look up.

"Hey. How're you feeling today?" I stepped up to her, announcing my arrival beforehand so as not to startle her.

I did anyway. Her head shot up, her eyes wide. "Oh. Jeremy. Hey."

"Got a lot on your mind?"

A sheepish smile. "Yeah."

"Haven't you got anyone to cover for you?" I glanced around. It was calm now, only one person sitting at a table reading and sipping a coffee.

"Not anyone out front. They've all got school." She stepped out from around the counter and motioned to the nearest table.

I took my seat opposite her. "You only employ school kids?"

"Out front yeah, though Leslie does the kitchen too. He goes to culinary school—and he's brilliant."

I smiled. "I did that too."

"You're a chef?" She beamed.

I nodded. "Working a shitty job though, so I don't feel like I'm challenged in the least. I'm going to start looking for a new one. The hours aren't great either. Lots of days off, which isn't very good for the economy."

"Well, if you need some extra shifts, I'm a bit short-staffed here at the moment. Saundra is about to pop her baby, so I don't know what to do once she does. The lads mostly works the evening shifts, what with them having school and all. So I'm out front a lot."

"You're not in the kitchen, yourself?"

"Well, I know how to make everything on the menu, and I can work the kitchen if it's an emergency. But I don't have any education, so I can't go around calling myself a chef." She cleared her voice and leaned forward. "Actually. The offer of shifts in the kitchen still stands. But when Chad gets out of hospital, I was thinking of offering him a few shifts a week out front. Do you think that would be a good idea?"

She was asking me advice about her nephew?

"I don't think I'm the right person to ask, but last I heard he has no interest returning to college, so getting shifts here will certainly give him something worthwhile to do with his time."

She nodded. "That's what I was thinking too. If he's up for it, anyway. You never know how the medicine's going to affect him. I hope they get it sorted while he's in hospital, but there're never any guarantees."

I was going to have to do my research on his

condition. I should power up the computer in the office when I got home and get to it before heading to work. The more I read up on, the better I'd understand what was going on or what to expect.

"Can I ask you..." Harriet trailed off as she played with a loose thread in her blouse. "What's the exact nature of your relationship with Chad? I know Dion was his teacher and you and Dion are a couple, but there's a lot more than that. Have either, or both of you, slept with him?"

Well, she was moving into the territory of Difficult Answers.

"As of yesterday, both of us." I found it best to be honest. I thought she was the kind of person to appreciate it, even if the subject was her nephew's sex life.

"He was hypersexual yesterday." She lifted her head, gaze searching mine.

"He was, yeah." Yesterday had just... happened. I'd been half-asleep and he'd been straddling me and it'd been good. I'd tried to push him away, to stop it, but he'd been pushing in just the right ways and it had, well, just happened.

I had no excuse. I'd known I was with Dion, that getting it on with Chad had been wrong, but I'd still allowed it to happen and it had been *good*.

"What about Dion? That happened before?"

This was even trickier. To tell the truth or not?

"I don't want you to think bad of him, because he only wants the best for Chad—"

"But he slept with Chad while he was still his teacher?" She interrupted me.

I pressed my lips together. "Yes. He reckons Chad was hypersexual and hallucinating at the time, too, but he didn't know that then."

Harriet nodded quickly. "Thank you for being honest with me. I appreciate that." She went back to fumbling with that lose thread.

It was distracting.

"What happens now though? He's in hospital, he's bipolar... what happens when he gets out? When he's better?" An *if he's better* hung unsaid in the air.

"We'll figure it out then. I mean, Dion really cares about him. More than me, because I don't know him very well. But, Harriet, I do care about him too and we'll figure it out. If he's willing to, that is."

I hoped he was. That his words and actions hadn't just been because his mania. Even if he wasn't willing to with me, he'd at least have Dion. I wasn't going to take Dion away from him.

Chad deserved all the happiness he could get, no matter what.

Harriet's gaze searched mine again. "Good." She

must've seen something she liked in them, because a small smile spread her lips. "I want to make it clear to him that, no matter what happens, he's always welcome with me too. I don't want him to run off if things don't work out with you."

"You think he would?"

"He's already shown he doesn't want to stay with me." That saddened her, which wasn't much of a surprise. I'd be worried if it hadn't. "But some people with bipolar… they tend to be flaky. Dad ran off several times, staying away for days or weeks at a time. Kendra did too, before she had Chad. After him, she seemed to be better, to have a purpose, until —" Her breath caught in her throat.

"I understand," I hurried to assure her, so she wouldn't have to say it. *Until she killed herself.*

It was a real tragedy, for both Harriet and especially for Chad—perhaps his dad too, maybe he'd been a better person before, but I kind of doubted that—to lose someone so loved. To lose them so young.

It made me long suddenly for my own parents. I hadn't spoken to them in weeks, not since before Dion had come home and told me he'd cheated on me.

I should rectify that by ringing mum up one day.

It wasn't like talking to either of them was a chore, after all.

They were loving parents who hadn't batted an eye when I'd told them I was gay. They adored Dion and thought I'd done a great catch.

I couldn't agree more.

Maybe they'd adore Chad too, if things worked out?

The door slammed open, the bell above it ringing furiously. I turned in time to see a flurry of movement as someone clad only in black came striding in, and then he stood in front of us, eyes black and furious.

Wynn.

Chad's friend.

And he didn't look at all happy.

CHAPTER 24

"Where the hell is Chad?" Wynn glanced between us, lips pressed tight. "Madison's funeral is right *now* and he's supposed to be there!"

"Wynn." Harriet stood slowly, palms out in a sign of peace. Or maybe this particular gesture was for *calm the fuck down* since he obviously needed to. "Chad's in hospital."

That brought him up short. "What? Why?"

"Because he was psychotic." Harriet stared at him, hard. "You never noticed anything weird about him? Sudden onset of mania or sudden crash into depression? Hallucinations, irritability, hypersexuality… Did you notice *nothing*?"

Wynn blinked once. "He's on drugs. There's side effects."

"He shouldn't be on drugs!" Harriet's voice was shrill. "Drugs and alcohol induce mania! He's fucking bipolar!"

Wynn shook his head sharply.

I noticed how blood-shot his eyes were and his hands weren't exactly steady. Having just lost his boyfriend, whom he clearly cared a great deal about, I could understand that he was upset and maybe not taking care of himself, but there was more than that.

His pupils were dilated.

"Harriet, *he*'s on drugs."

She sniffled. "Of course he is. He gives them to Chad all the time, why shouldn't he use them himself?"

Wynn's eyes narrowed dangerously, and without preamble he reached out and shoved Harriet hard.

"What the fuck do you know? I've been there for Chad through everything while you've been absent. I've been helping him deal with things the best way he can—and if that's through drugs then so be it! Not everyone's such a fucking prude, not everyone's able to cope with things without some fucking help!"

I'd jumped up the minute he'd shoved her, but he didn't seem inclined to do so again.

He was seething though, so I didn't trust him at all.

If he lunged for Harriet again, I was ready this time.

"Therapy is a lot more healthy way to deal with things." Harriet cradled her arms in front of her chest. Maybe she was afraid of being pushed again, or maybe she was just feeling vulnerable. Both, perhaps. "Therapy is what he needs. It went so far that he pulled a knife on himself! They had to restrain him! He's being admitted by force because he's a danger to himself and to others, and it could've been avoided if only he'd got help earlier!"

She cried now, her small, thin body wracked by sobs.

I brushed past Wynn to wrap my arms around her.

She fell against my chest, crying.

The only other customer in the Café was looking at us side-ways, his coffee cup halfway to his lips and forgotten about.

The woman who worked in the kitchen was now in the doorway too, eyes wide as she took in the scene in front of her.

"You know nothing about what Chad needs," Wynn snarled. "I've been his friend for *years*. You've never been around."

"I've never been *allowed* to! And he never wanted to be around *me*!"

"Harriet, *shhh*, calm down." I rubbed her back, trying to soothe her.

Wynn's presence wasn't of any help, with his glaring daggers at her.

"Chad was supposed to be at Madison's funeral, because I'm not bloody *allowed* to be. He was supposed to be there!" His voice broke, and just like that I realised how much he was hurting too.

He'd lost one of the people closest to him, and to be refused to be present in the funeral as well... that couldn't feel any good.

I couldn't even imagine losing Dion and be refused to say my last goodbye by his family.

Most of all because I'd never met his family, but also because it was such a far off thing. I couldn't even imagine the grief felt by losing someone who'd been so close to you.

Wynn stared at Harriet for another half minute. Then he turned on his heels and stalked right back out again. The door slammed so hard the glass rattled after him.

Harriet was still sobbing.

"Come on, Harriet, calm down. He's gone now." I steered her back to her chair, pushed her down, then wiped the tears away from her splotched cheeks, and reached out for some napkins for her to clean herself up with.

She dabbed them at her eyes, tears soaking into the paper. "I know he's hurting, I *do*, but he should've seen the signs better than anyone."

"It's not easy though, is it? If he's on drugs… Chad, I mean. Drugs can have the same side-effects as the symptoms of bipolar." As far as I knew, anyway. Hallucinations or delusions at least, I'd heard of people on drugs having them.

People had died because of it, because they'd believed they could fly and jumped out a window or over a bridge.

Oh God.

Has Chad ever had those kinds of delusions?

"I know. I know that." Harriet blew her nose. "It's just… It's so hard. Chad should've seen someone, a psychiatrist, right after his mum died. They would've caught on, if it even happened that early."

I pressed my lips tight, Chad's admission about what exactly had happened after his mother died ringing loud and clear in my mind.

If he'd been able to see someone, maybe he never would've let himself be taken advantage of by a paedophile preying on hurting young boys.

But I also remembered how angry he'd been when neither Dion nor I had understood that it and been a good experience for him, so I suppose it was something better left buried until, or if, he realised otherwise.

It certainly wasn't something Harriet needed to know about.

It was Chad's secret, Chad's life.

It would also serve to make her feel even more guilty, and it wasn't worth it. Not when Chad thought it had been *good*. That the priest had been a good man taking care of him.

Harriet kept sniffling for a while and occasionally dabbed at her eyes or blew her nose again.

The bell jingled, announcing someone entering in a calm, proper manner.

"Dammit," I heard her mutter, pressing a new napkin to her eyes again.

"Want me to help you out for a bit? I can do that." How difficult could it be being out front, right?

"Would you mind?" She sounded choked up again.

"Not at all."

I MET Dion first when I finished work that night.

He was relaxing on the sofa, with a football game on the telly. Not that I thought he was actually paying any attention to it, because his head rested against the back of the sofa and he seemed deep in thought.

"Hey." I sunk down next to him and scooted closer so we were touching.

He instantly wrapped his arm around my shoulder, like he'd always done before.

I liked that we were back to it again.

"Hard evening?"

"Hard day." I preceded to tell him what had happened at the Café.

"Well, our lives have certainly become interesting."

I snorted a laughter. "Yeah. What'd we do before?"

"I think a general day consisted of work, dinner, and then ended with us on the sofa, watching the telly before bed. Not exactly the most exciting life."

"We didn't complain either, though." I put my head on his shoulder, enjoying the feel of him close and the smell of his aftershave.

He was silent a moment. "Are you really okay with things? What we talked about yesterday?"

"Yeah." *Hopefully. I think.* "You've been thinking about him all day, haven't you?"

He sighed. "I keep wondering what it must be like for him, being locked up now. He's never had anyone setting any sort of boundaries for him. He's always been able to go where he wanted and do what he wanted. He can't do that now, I keep wondering how he feels about it. Is he relieved to finally get help? Or does he resent it?"

All valid questions.

"I hope we get to see him soon. I want to make sure he *is* doing better, that being in hospital *is* helpful." His arms tightened around me and he turned his head to look me right in the eyes. "I'm sorry I dragged all this on you. You were happy before, and I messed it up."

"I can be happy now too." I cupped his cheek in one hand and stroked my thumb over his skin. "Change is good sometimes. I hope this is one of them."

His other arm came up and he tangled his fingers in my hair, tilting my head just so. "I hope so too."

When he kissed me, it was slow and chaste and full of hope—and it was *good*.

DION GOT to see Chad the next day, but I had to work another late shift.

Bloody typical.

I was in a foul mood all day, because I'd wanted

to see Chad too. And a small part of me was a bit jealous that just the two of them got to spend time together. I tried to squash that feeling though, but it kept rearing its ugly head all evening as I imagined what they could be doing together.

It couldn't be much, considering Chad was still in hospital, but it grated all the same.

Dion sat with his head in his hands when I got home, and my foul mood was replaced with something else.

Fright.

"What's wrong?" I hurried over to him.

"He wasn't responding to the medicine, so he got all psychotic. They had to put him in restraints again."

"Bloody hell." I rubbed a hand over Dion's shoulders, trying to soothe him. "What happened?"

"He seemed normal at first. He smiled when I arrived. But then he started muttering things I couldn't catch and then he got angry. I think he had auditory hallucinations—and they weren't good ones. He lashed out and the staff came rushing in. They forced him down flat on the bed and restrained him, and all the while he was shouting and screaming and fighting them. It was horrible."

I stopped rubbing and instead hugged him. "Was Harriet there?"

A minuscule nod. "She reckons he'd got too low a dosage of antipsychotic. Which means they have to up it."

"Isn't that good? If it makes him come down, I mean?"

"I don't know." Dion sighed. "Those are pretty strong drugs, you know. I worry about side-effects if the dosage gets too high. I read up on stuff at work today, and there can be lots of side-effects to the medicines."

"If they find the right dosage for him then it can't be so bad?"

"I don't think so. But it's the process of actually finding the right dosage that's tricky."

Yeah, I could imagine it couldn't be easy. But then again, the doctors were trained for it. They couldn't be wrong many times before they got it right.

"So now he's back to not being allowed visitors for a few days. I don't think we'll get to see him over the weekend."

"Then I think we should get away for the weekend."

He looked at me, startled. "Away? Where?"

"We could go up and visit my parents. It's been a while since we've seen them now."

He blinked. "And tell them what?"

"Nothing." I stared back. "There's nothing to tell.

We need to figure out things ourselves first before we drag them into it. They don't need to know anything until we're certain. And if it doesn't work out, they don't ever need to know at all." I put my hand on his stomach, feeling the taut muscles. "They might not mind me being gay or us being together, but I don't think they'll be as open-minded if they find out about our current situation."

"Yeah, I guess you're right." He kissed my temple. "I suppose it is time to go see them. I've missed them."

"Me too." I leaned further into him. "And when we get back, hopefully we can see Chad again." Maybe he'd be back on his feet by that time, if the doctors managed to keep him from rising to a manic state.

I sure hoped we'd get to see him, no matter what.

It was time to figure things out.

CHAPTER 25

*C*had was sitting up in bed when we entered his room on Monday morning.

Dion had taken the morning off, and I... well, I had another day of no work ahead of me.

He sat cross-legged on the bed, bent over a sketchbook. The pencil flew over the page. It didn't seem like the morning at the funeral though, when he'd been so intent on his drawing he hadn't even wanted to have breakfast. The drawing then had been so quick—and he'd changed the page before he'd even finished a sketch.

Dion knocked softly on the doorway, which startled Chad nonetheless.

His head shot up, his eyes were wide, but then softened as he smiled sheepishly.

"Hey. How are you feeling?" Dion walked directly over to him, while I hovered back a bit.

I didn't know what to do now I was actually *there* facing him.

"Better." Chad closed the sketchbook with careful movements and put it on the table at the side of the bed. His eyes flickered to me. "Hi."

"Hi." I stepped further into the room, stopping at the bottom of the bed.

Chad's cheeks were red when he turned back to Dion. "Could you give us a minute?"

He frowned in confusion. "I'll be just outside."

I looked after him until he was gone then turned back to Chad, who stared down at his folded hands. I swallowed, nervous now we were alone.

That he'd even asked Dion to leave us so we *could* be alone.

What does he want with me?

He glanced up, but when he saw I was already looking at him, he bowed his head again. "I'm so sorry," he whispered.

"For what?" That surprised me. He didn't have anything to apologise before. It wasn't his fault he was sick.

"I forced you into sex and I never should've done that."

"Oh. *That.*" I left my place at the foot of the bed

and sat down precariously on the bed next to him. "You didn't force me. You were a bit force*ful* perhaps, but I was a willing participant."

"No, you weren't. You kept trying to push me away." He gripped onto his trousers, bunching the loose fabric. "And I kept thinking that of course you'd want me, that everyone wanted me. But you didn't. You mentioned Dion. And yet I continued to push and you let it happen."

"I did. I did let it happen." I remembered his flushed face, his mouth on my skin, his cock against mine. It hadn't been an unpleasant experience at all. "But I liked it, Chad. I gave up fighting, because it felt *good*."

The redness in his cheeks had receded a bit. "I still shouldn't have done it in the first place. It's just, sometimes, I *need* sex and I do stupid things to get it. Like force you. And I assaulted this bloke in the Café, Harriet's girlfriend's son. It didn't even occur to me that he didn't want to. *I* wanted to, and that was all that mattered."

I clapped his shoulder lamely, feeling uncomfortably antsy all of a sudden. "That was all it was? The disorder? That's the only reason you did it?" Maybe there was no chance for the three of us, after all. Maybe I'd just have to deal with both of us having Dion.

"It makes me do stupid things." He rubbed his forehead. "You know, I didn't even know about Mum. All I remember was she killed herself. I didn't know she had a mental disorder. I just thought *I* was going mental."

I stopped my patting—it was a stupid thing to do anyway—and instead gripped his opposite shoulder tightly.

Dion stuck his head around the doorway and I motioned for him to come inside with my free hand. He did so hesitantly, glancing between us.

"I wasn't on drugs all those times, I swear." I wasn't sure Chad even realised Dion was back in the room, as he still had his head bowed. "Wynn thought I was, Dion thought I was, you probably thought I was. But I wasn't. I took drugs when I was at Wynn's place, but they were out of my system by the time I came back to yours."

"I believe you." I squeezed his shoulders. "Harriet said drugs induce mania."

Dion crouched down in front of him, which earned him a startled look from Chad. "I'm sorry I jumped to conclusions. Not just now while you've been staying with us, but back in college too. I just... I thought it was drugs." He took Chad's clenched hands in his, forcing them apart and caressing the back of them tenderly.

Chad leaned into the touch. Away from mine.

I let my hand fall uselessly to the bed. I was, perhaps a bit too surprisingly, disappointed.

"I'm going to go find something to drink."

I hightailed it out of there, looking frantically around for a shop or a vendor. If Chad wanted to be with just Dion, I would have to get used to the two of them spending some time alone.

I couldn't always be present, not when it seemed Chad didn't want me there.

Had I been *that* keen on the three of us together? Must've been, considering how disappointed I felt now.

It was pathetic really.

I didn't even know Chad.

What I did know were things I'd learned and seen while he'd been manic or depressed.

I wasn't sure I'd ever seen him in a normal mood.

Looking back now, knowing about the disorder, it was difficult to tell. The manic moments were easy to pinpoint, such as that walk we'd had, the sex, and the day of the funeral.

And the ones where he'd been very depressed too, especially the days he couldn't even get out of bed.

But in-between those two extremes... I wasn't

sure if he'd still been in a mood or if he'd been normal then.

No matter what it was, I *was* charmed by him. I did find him handsome and I did feel sorry for him, and everything was just so jumbled.

Only thing that was certain was that Chad wanted Dion, and Dion wanted Chad.

He also wanted me, which seemed to be leading to an open relationship.

I wasn't sure I even wanted that.

Could I share Dion with someone else? All of us being together was a better thought, left a better feeling.

If we had to share, I was afraid jealousy would eat at me. But maybe it would if we were all together too.

I didn't know. I'd never been in this situation before. This difficult situation.

I found a vendor eventually. I fed it some money and it gave me a cold soft drink to enjoy. Only I didn't feel like enjoying anything at the moment.

Leaning against the side of the vendor, I tilted my head up to look at the ceiling.

Could this even work out?

I didn't know anyone who'd ever been in a three-way relationship, or people who's open relationship had survived the trials and struggles it brought.

I rubbed my face. I wasn't prepared to lose Dion. Two years in, and I knew I wanted to be with him.

Even if he had cheated on me.

Then again, I'd ended up cheating on him too.

With Chad.

It all came down to him, really.

If we hit it off, if all three of us would be together or if we'd just share Dion between us.

Share Dion *and* share a flat?

I was dubious about that.

It wouldn't work out, would it?

Or would there be less jealousy if we were all living in the same space?

Then again, what would Dion do if we were all spending time together? Cuddle us on each side? God, that wasn't ideal *at all*.

I pushed away from the vendor and headed back to Chad's room.

Dion had taken my place next to him, with his arm around Chad's shoulders, and Chad leaning into him.

"They say I've got rapid cycling bipolar," Chad was muttering. "That's the most difficult one to treat, because the mood swings are so sudden. They say it could only be from stress though, and that when things calm down it might be I'm not rapid cycling anymore."

"Whatever it is, we'll figure it out." Dion sounded certain.

I wasn't sure he was, deep down, but for now he sounded it.

That was what Chad needed, probably. He needed someone to be strong for him.

I didn't think that could be Harriet, not at the moment. She was crushed from everything. Maybe not from Chad's dad's death, but from finding out about the abuse and Chad's illness.

Chad sniffled. "I didn't get to go to Madison's funeral. Wynn's going to kill me."

"Why's that?"

"Because he's not allowed to go. Madison's mum isn't a very nice person. She said if he came, she'd have him forcefully removed."

I finally entered the room. "I don't think it's going to be anything that drastic. Wynn will understand." I think he had, he'd calmed down about Chad attending the funeral once he'd found out he was in hospital, though he'd still been furious at life in general.

Chad looked up at me, eyes brimming with tears. "Will you check on him? He's alone now. His mum doesn't care. And last time I was over, he was snorting coke, and Wynn doesn't *do* drugs. He sells them, but he doesn't use them, but now he *does*, and I'm so scared he'll do something stupid."

I nodded quickly. "Of course I will." I knew where he lived. Our meeting outside his flat was still loud and clear in my mind.

"Will you do it now?" Chad's eyes were wide, begging me to do as he wished. "I have a bad feeling. Please."

"Yeah. Okay." I glanced at Dion, who seemed conflicted. "You stay here. I won't be long."

He seemed more relieved.

Something stabbed at my heart.

Thanks, he seemed to tell me with his eyes.

I took a deep breath and started to turn around, but then Chad was suddenly off the bed and around my neck, hugging me tightly.

"Thankyou, thankyou, *thankyou*!"

I wondered if he was manic again as I hesitantly slid my own arms around his back. "It's no problem. Really. He's your best friend, he just lost someone important to him. Of course someone should go check up on him."

Chad seemed reluctant to let go of me, but once he did he rocked back of his feet as he looked up at me shyly. He licked his lips, which my eyes zeroed in on without my permission, but then he bowed his head and slunk back to the bed.

"I'll just go then," I said lamely, and walked out before either of them could answer.

I had to top up my Oyster card on the tube, which was quicker for this trip than taking the bus. I preferred the tube, anyway, as the bus could take over twice as long as a quick trip on the tube.

The tube was more expensive, though, which was why I didn't take it often.

I really *did* need to get a better job that also gave me a higher salary. Dion was the one with the high, steady income—as high as it came for teachers anyway—and so he paid more rent than I did, though we tried to split it equal. It was just some months I didn't have the money to pay half of everything.

Harriet's offer of shifts at the Café was tempting. At least I could help her out there while she needed me, while at the same time looking for a full-time job that I could see myself in for a while. I couldn't see myself at my current job or at the Café, for that matter, it wasn't my style.

But I could do it temporarily.

I reached Wynn's street and saw a light up in the flat I assumed was his. I took the stairs, my thighs burning at the top of them since I wasn't used to climbing that many stairs, and knocked on the door.

There was no answer, no sounds coming from inside.

Chad's bad feeling started to settle in my stomach now too, as my second knock didn't bring about any sounds either.

I tried the knob, certain it would be locked, but holding out hope.

Turned out the door swung open without so much as a creak.

What met me inside made the bad feeling plummet into horror.

CHAPTER 26

*T*he smell hit me first; smell of vomit.

And then I saw the lifeless form on the sofa.

Oh, God, no.

Don't let him lose his best friend too!

I hurried over and checked Wynn's neck for a pulse. He had one, but it took me a minute to find, and it was weak.

I pulled my mobile phone out of my jacket pocket and quickly dialled the emergency number. I had them saying directions in my ear as I checked Wynn over and rolled him into the correct position, so he wouldn't choke on his own vomit.

There were drugs on the table. An empty syringe too.

Jesus.

I didn't know what they were, but maybe the ambulance personnel would? Or maybe they'd even bring it to the hospital with them for the doctors to recognise. I had no idea about the procedure of these things.

It didn't take long for the ambulance personnel to arrive.

I stepped out of the way as they crowded around Wynn.

"Are you family?" One of them asked, not looking at me, but it was obvious the question was directed my way.

"No, I was just coming to check on him for a friend."

"We have to get him to the hospital ASAP," the other one said, and with that they moved him onto the gurney they'd brought with them upstairs.

"Which hospital?" I asked, hoping it would be the one Chad was in.

It wasn't.

They shuffled Wynn off on the gurney, leaving me inside the flat confused as to what to do now. I couldn't just leave it unlocked, else he would find himself robbed off everything he owned. Which meant I needed to locate a key.

That wasn't hard, actually, as it lay in a bowl by the door.

But the smell... Vomit was all over the sofa.

I wasn't sure it was even salvageable at this point, but if I left it as it was, the smell would be even worse when—*if*—Wynn did come home. So I tried to clean it up as best as I could, and I opened windows for fresh air.

I locked the door once I left, and then headed to the hospital.

Not to Chad and Dion—but to check on Wynn.

"He hasn't got any family that cares," I told the nurse when she didn't want to tell me anything. "I'm here for a friend of mine, who's also in hospital, and he needs to know how his best friend is doing."

The nurse was still tight-lipped, so I settled on a chair to wait.

Wynn's keys dug into my palm as I clenched my fingers around them.

I didn't know if what Chad had said was true. Did Wynn really have *no one*? Didn't he have parents, at the very least?

Maybe they don't care.

That was a possibility. Not everyone had as good of parents as I had. Many had crappy parents, and I only had to look as far as to both Dion and Chad to confirm that.

I didn't know how long I sat there.

My phone vibrated in my pocket and I knew it was Dion, but I couldn't take it and tell him I didn't know anything. He was with Chad and if Chad found out his best friend was in hospital overdosed on drugs...

I didn't know how frail his mind was.

Maybe it would spiral him right back into the rapid cycling he'd been speaking about. I didn't want that.

At the same time, if I didn't answer my phone, maybe they'd both think the worst?

It stopped ringing and I instantly rang back, regretting not answering now. "Hey," I said once Dion answered.

"Where are you?"

"Hospital." I glanced up at the nurse who refused to tell me anything, but she seemed busy.

"So you'll be right up then?"

"I'm at A&E, Dion. Wynn... Chad was right in his bad feeling. He overdosed. I don't know if he's alive or dead, because no one will tell me anything."

Dion drew in a sharp breath and I heard Chad say something in the background.

"I'm waiting here now. I hope they'll tell me something eventually. As I'm not family, I'm not privy to information. But Chad said he doesn't have anyone else, so… here I am."

"Ring when you know something more, okay?" And with that Dion hung up.

I didn't envy him having to explain it to Chad.

What'll happen with him now?

If he'd been rapid cycling because of stress, another person in his life dying would definitely add to that.

What a crappy hand in life he'd been given.

VISITING hours were over by the time I got back to Chad's room, but a kind nurse let me in anyway.

She seemed to know about the situation, as she asked me how it'd gone. I told her then walked into Chad's room, where he was lying flat on his bed.

"Jeremy!" He sat up so fast I was afraid he'd get a crick in his back. "Dion had to go. They wouldn't let him stay."

"I know." I sat down on the edge.

He swallowed heavily, gaze searching my face. "Is he… dead?"

"No." At least I came travelling with good news. "No, he's not. It was critical for a while, but they managed to get him back. They seemed to think he'd done it deliberately, so he's being sectioned once he's recovered from the overdose itself."

Chad's entire face showed relief. "Oh God!" He bent over, resting his face against his knees. He was shaking. "I was so afraid. I thought he'd—"

"I know." I rubbed his back. "But he's not. He's alive. He's not well, but he's alive. He'll get help too now."

Chad nodded jerkily, but kept his bent over position for a while.

"Excuse me, Mr. Layton." The nurse stuck her head around the door. "I can't allow you to stay much longer."

I nodded my understanding. "Let me just say goodbye?"

She smiled and disappeared, and I turned back to Chad, who'd started straightening up again now. His eyes were tearful, and that was all the warning I got before he was around my neck again.

I hugged him tight without hesitation this time.

"I don't want you to leave," he mumbled against my neck. "I hate being here. I want to be back with you."

"Once you're better, they'll let you out. *Then* you can come stay with us." I stroked his back, feeling the ridges of his spine through the thin shirt he wore. "Just focus on getting better. Make sure you've got the right dose of medicine, and once you're ready we'll be here."

He drew in several shaky breaths, and I worried he was going to start crying on me. He didn't, but I was sure he barely managed to keep the tears back. He held onto me so tight I wondered if I might get bruises, but as long as he felt comforted in the end, it was worth it.

When he did let go off me, he was subdued.

"I'll be back tomorrow, okay? Both Dion and I will." I squeezed his shoulder before standing. "As long as they allow visitors, we'll be here every day, if you want."

"I do," he said quickly. "I do want you to come. Both of you."

Okay, that warmed. "I'll see you tomorrow then."

I left him there on the bed, sitting cross-legged and looking after me.

His admission of not wanting me to leave gnawed at me all the way home, but the nurse wouldn't have allowed me to stay anyway, so it shouldn't have. It was just the despair in his voice when he'd said it…

"Smells good in here," I said once I entered the flat.

Dion came walking out of the kitchen. "I'm making us curry."

"You're the chef in this relationship now?" I

teased as I stepped in close to him so I could wrap my arms around his torso.

"I try." He embraced me in return and we hugged for a long minute. "How was he when you got there to see him?"

"Relieved that Wynn was alive." I buried my face in Dion's neck, breathing in his subtle cologne. "Didn't want me to leave him there."

"He asked about you, you know." Dion's grip around me tightened.

"Oh? When?"

"When you left the room to get something to drink. He didn't think you liked him."

"What did you say?"

"Well, I didn't get a chance to say anything as you came back. But when you left to check on Wynn, I reassured him that you *did*. I told him what you told me, about how the three of us could try and figure out how to be together?" He was hesitant now, as if he didn't think he'd been allowed to mention that.

"Good." It was my turn to squeeze him tighter.

"So you're absolutely certain this is what you want?"

"Not absolutely, no." I drew back so I could look up at him. "But I want to try. It might work out. If it doesn't… then we'll deal with it then."

Dion carded a hand through my hair, gaze

roaming my face. It made me feel a bit self-conscious, but also good. "He said he *did* like you."

"Chad did?" It surprised me.

Earlier in the day I'd thought he didn't, but then now he hadn't wanted me to leave… but that could've just been because he didn't want to be alone. But he had also said he'd wanted me to come visit him every day too.

"I assume that's why you up and left the room, because you thought he didn't."

I frowned up at him.

He smiled in return. "We've been together a while, you know, I can read you like an open book."

"Reckon that, do you?" I dug my fingers into his side playfully, knowing he was ticklish there.

He chuckled. "I do. And it feels so good that we can be like this around each other again. I've missed you these weeks." His gaze searched mine. For what, I didn't know.

"I've missed you too." I leaned in to kiss him lightly. "But if you ever cheat on me again with someone else—someone who's not Chad—I promise I won't be so forgiving."

His arms slid around my waist. "That won't happen. I swear. It's only you—and Chad."

My hands locked around his biceps, holding them tight. "Good."

"That goes for you too, you know."

"I never wanted anyone but you," I protested. "Well. And then Chad, apparently. But yeah, only us. No one else. No open relationship where we can go shag whomever we want."

"I have no need to shag whoever I want, as long as I can shag you." His hands inched down to cup my bum, fingers squeezing me.

It sent a jolt of lust straight through me and my breath caught in my throat.

He hardened up against me, and so did I against him.

Sex, sex, sex.

My brain switched gears instantly and it was all I could think about.

"What about the curry?" My voice came out strangled.

"I'll turn off the cooker. We can heat it up later." Dion left me standing there, all kinds of needy, but he was back a minute later, pressing up against me. "I've missed you so much."

I tangled my fingers in his hair as he turned me around and pushed me up against the wall.

His lips descended on mine, all hard and demanding, and *bloody hell* but I melted from it. It'd been too long since we'd been intimate.

His tongue invaded my mouth. The stubble on his jaw scratched my smooth-shaven one.

The wall was hard against my back.

He was hard against my front.

I fumbled for his zipper and the minute I got it up, I thrust my hand down his underwear.

He bucked against me, a groan erupting from deep in his throat.

"Let's take this to the bedroom." The bedroom that had been out of use for a great many weeks.

Or maybe not, considering Chad and I had taken the bed to use only days ago.

But it'd been a while for Dion and I.

Now it was finally happening.

I longed for it like I longed to breathe, and when he pushed me down on the bed, I was all too happy to let him ravish me.

CHAPTER 27

"*W*hat are we supposed to do when Chad comes back?"

I'd been dozing on my side, but now I rolled onto my back and tilted my head to look at Dion.

He was on his back too, the duvet pooling at his hips, hiding one leg and his groin from view. Everything else was bared for the world to see. If the world could look inside our bedroom, anyway.

"What do you mean?"

Dion stared resolutely up at the ceiling. "Is he supposed to stay in the guest room again?"

Oh, he's getting into that subject.

"I don't know. I haven't even thought that far ahead. I suppose… if we're all going to be together, we should all share a bedroom too? Or if not, we could alternate nights here in the double bed with you."

He grimaced. "That doesn't sound right. Me being shared by the two of you on opposite days. Sounds like those polygamist blokes you hear about who spends one night a week in each of his wives' beds."

"It might be a possibility, you know. If Chad and I aren't together, we can't be sharing a bed either." I put my hand on his upper stomach, over his ribs. "Besides, it wouldn't be like that."

"That's exactly what it would be like, and I don't like it."

"But you want both of us. What're you going to do then if we don't want each other?" I inched over to put my chin on his shoulder too. "Then it *is* going to be like that."

"You know, Jem, it never occurred to me to even propose a threeway relationship. The thought only stuck because you brought it up, and now I think about it... it's not at all bad. I get what I want, and hopefully you both get something you hadn't realised you'd been wanting." He smiled self-consciously. "God, does that sound selfish? It does, doesn't it, but it's the truth. I *do* want both of you."

I watched my hand move slowly up from his

stomach to his chest, settling over the course, dark-blond hair.

"Do you think it's possible to love two people at the same time?"

I drew in a breath. Both surprised at the question and not knowing what to answer. "Before I would've said no. But watching you with Chad, how you care about him… and I know you love me. So yes, I *do* think it's possible."

He turned over on his side so abruptly our foreheads almost knocked together.

I pulled back a bit so we were nose to nose instead.

"Do you think *you* could love two people?"

"Again, before I would've said no, but now… I do care about him, Dion, even though most of what I've seen in him so far is his disorder. But he's a sweet lad and he needs someone there for him, and yes, I want to be that person. I *want* him. If I hadn't, I never would've let him seduce me in the first place."

Dion's arm slid around my face, bringing me in closer. Only the duvet kept us from being pressed up skin to skin.

"Is it weird that I *like* the thought of you two together? When you first told me, I wasn't happy, I'll admit that. But now… it's a turn-on."

I pushed his shoulder playfully. "Maybe if

anything does happen in the future, we'll let you watch."

"I wouldn't be opposed to that." He kissed me, though it wasn't the passionate kiss from earlier. This was slow and chaste, but still oh-so-good. "I am sorry, though, for pushing all this on you. For cheating on you to begin with. It was never my intention to actually sleep with him."

"Even if you wanted to?"

Searching gaze. "I did, yeah."

"You've already told me you were sorry." I cupped a stubbled cheek in my palm. "And I was angry. I was real mad at you. But then Chad showed up and suddenly—I wasn't anymore. And then I went and did what I'd been angry at you for in the first place."

"You had every right to be angry. I would've been too, if the situation had been reversed."

I snuggled in close to him, still sated from the sex and happy we were finally back to where we'd been before everything got so messed up.

"You're right though. Adjusting to having Chad here when he gets out of hospital is going to be a challenge. It's going to be weird to get used to the fact he's a proper part of our lives."

"Yeah." Dion sighed. "I hope it's going to be good though. I mean, most of my knowledge with him is from college. And while he was here, his mood was swinging rapidly. I'm not sure he was ever himself while he was here."

I wasn't sure either, but then I didn't know what he was like when he was *himself*.

Had he been himself today or had he switched from mania to depression?

If anything, I was excited about what was going to happen. If it turned out well, anyway. If it didn't, my excitement would wane pretty damn fast.

I could only hope it didn't.

YESTERDAY'S MOOD must've been the normal, because Chad was clearly depressed when we popped in for a visit the next day.

He was in bed, under the duvet, and he didn't even turn his head to look at us or greet us.

"I brought you some curry." Left-overs from the dinner Dion had made, which had actually been quite good, even if it'd been heated up and eaten as breakfast today instead. "Thought you might like something other than hospital food."

No answer.

No movement.

I exchanged a glance with Dion, who went over to

the other side of the bed where he faced Chad. "You not feeling all right today?"

"They won't let me out to see Wynn." I almost missed what he said, his voice was so low. But I did catch it, even barely, and my stomach tightened up in knots.

I'd forgotten about Wynn already.

My thoughts were so set on Dion and Chad, everything that had happened and likely would happen, that I'd forgotten all about Chad's best friend and the precarious state he was in.

"I want to go see him, make sure he's all right, but they won't let me."

"You have to get better first." Dion reached out to brush away some auburn strands from Chad's forehead. "They can't let you out while you're rapid cycling and a danger to yourself and others."

"I'm not anymore, though," he protested weakly. "I just want to check on Wynn. Then I want to sleep."

I put the lidded box of curry on the bedside table and went around the bed to stand at Dion's side.

When he realised we both could see him, he resolutely turned his head the other way.

"I want to be alone."

I exchanged another glance with Dion.

"All right. We'll be back tomorrow, okay? Maybe you're feeling better then." Dion bent down and placed a brief kiss on Chad's temple then quickly shot a guilty look my way.

Which wasn't at all necessary was it, as we'd talked about it. We'd figured things out.

Mostly.

"Please eat the curry when you feel up for it." I settled for squeezing his shoulder, not at all comfortable doing anything more intimate. Besides the sex, we hadn't been close, and that had happened because he'd been hypersexual.

He didn't say anything as we left.

"Oh, hey!" Harriet met us in the hallway. She looked better today, more cheerful and not like she had the world's burden weighting down her shoulders. "You've been in to see him? Well, obviously." She grinned sheepishly. "You're just exiting his room."

"You've just arrived?" I asked, casting a quick look back at the door to Chad's room.

"Yeah."

"He's depressed today." I felt she was due the warning, what with her good mood and all. "We didn't even get to stay two minutes."

Her smile fell a fraction. "It is to be expected. He can't be on anti-depressants, because they induce the mania, so the depression has to be managed with mood stabilisers, and there too they have to find the right dosage."

"You know a lot about this," Dion commented.

She smiled, somewhat bitterly. "I grew up with it, remember? First my dad and then Kendra. It's childhood knowledge for me, though now they have better medicines than they had back then."

"I do hope they start working soon." Dion put his hands on the small of his back, presumably to stop them from fumbling around. He did that sometimes when he didn't know what to do with them.

"Me too. Takes time though, but I do believe the antipsychotic medicine is working. Now it's about finding the right dosage to manage the depressive episodes." Harriet smiled at both of us. "I'll see if I have better luck with him."

"We'll be back tomorrow," Dion promised.

We both lifted our hands in a wave as we parted.

"You all right?" Dion asked the minute we were out in fresh air.

"Yeah. Shouldn't I be?" I raised my eyebrows in surprised question.

"I don't know." He shrugged. "Just that kiss."

"I know you've been far more intimate with him than that chaste kiss," I said drily.

"Yeah, but this was the first time you saw it. I don't know… maybe you felt something unexpected?

Like, you don't want to go through with this after all?"

I hadn't really felt anything. I'd felt sorry for Chad, and worried. But other than that…

"It's fine, Dion. We're going to have to get used to it, without feeling guilty every time one of us touch another in front of one another."

He grabbed me around the neck and pulled me in to place a kiss on *my* temple. "You're amazing, you know that right?"

"Well, I try." We'd never been overly fond of public displays of affection, but I allowed the kiss to my temple because really, it wasn't anything anyone could take offence to.

Not that I minded if anyone took offence to me snogging my boyfriend in public, but my relationship was a private thing, and I liked to keep it private.

"I have to go back to work." Dion had skipped out to go to the hospital.

"I've got the late shift. Will you be up when I get home?"

"Can't promise, but I'll try." He let his hand drop from my neck. It seemed reluctant and it made me happy. Even if Chad was in the picture, he still wanted me. I'd had that proven the day before with the hot sex, but to have it proven in an innocent way, like this, was good too.

"If not, I'll see you tomorrow." He walked away, the opposite direction from the way home.

I decided not to go home though, but to head off to check up on Wynn. Maybe if Chad knew how his friend was doing, he'd be doing better too.

Not that I got much information out of the nurses.

I learned he was still alive—which was always a good thing—and had been admitted to hospital for an extended period of time, but only family was allowed to visit and since I didn't belong in that category, I didn't get to see him.

Not that he had any family to care about him, but the nurses wouldn't listen to that.

So I went home. Spent a few hours diddling about, updating my CV and looking for available jobs. Then it was time to head off to the one job I hated more than anything else.

All the time I kept thinking about Chad and his friend; the decision I'd made regarding Chad, Dion and I; and how in the world we were going to make it work when Chad had been a previous student of Dion's and someone I didn't really know at all.

But we'd work it out.

We *had* to.

CHAPTER 28

I was cooking an exquisite dinner, just to prove to myself that I could do fancy food still, but also because I wanted Dion and I to have a nice, special evening.

We didn't do dates; a good dinner at home with a glass of wine or two was as far as we went.

"Smells like heaven," he proclaimed when he got home from work.

"Hope it tastes the same too." I knew it would. I'd already had a taste. I was confident in my abilities too, which was why my shitty job was such a personal tragedy.

But it was all I'd been able to find on short notice, after the restaurant I'd worked in previously had been shut down when the owners retired.

"I'll just have a quick shower then I'll be right out."

"No hurry." The food wasn't near finished yet. I'd only heated the skillet for the filets mignons, and was now seasoning them with salt and pepper before they were ready to be cooked.

The ring of the bell sounded through the flat before I could put the meat on the skillet, which was just as good, as it was only going to cook for maximum seven minutes on each side.

I grabbed a wad of paper to dry my hands off then hurried over to the door.

Who could be ringing on our door? It wasn't like we knew anyone that tended to simply pop over for a visit.

It wasn't just anyone standing out there.

It was Chad.

"Hey." I let out on a surprised breath. He had a bag at his feet, was dressed in loose-fitting jeans and a thin jumper underneath an open jacket. His face was devoid of any trace of bruises, like it'd been for a while now. It also held an expression I could only describe as nervous.

"Hey." He bit down on his lower lip, but his green gaze was locked on me.

"I didn't think you'd get out till tomorrow?" That

was what he'd said when I'd stopped by earlier in the day.

It was what he'd said the last three days, as well.

"I got out early for good behaviour." A cheeky grin passed his lips then he was back to that nervous lip-biting. "I'm—I'm still welcome, right?"

"Of course!" I all but jumped away from the door so he could come inside.

He picked up his bag, brushed past me, then dropped it to the floor and whirled around to face me again. "If you don't want me here, just say so. I can go stay with Harriet. She's offered that at least once a day, so…"

"I do," I assured him, closing the door with a firm gesture. "Of course I do." I nodded my head towards the kitchen. "Come on, I'm cooking. Good thing I always make a lot of food. I wasn't expecting you today."

A sheepish smile passed his lips as he trailed after me.

The shower was running, so Dion would be a while still.

That left me to entertain him, and suddenly having him around felt extremely awkward. I'd been preparing myself for *tomorrow*, not today.

"What're you making?" He eyed the seasoned meat.

"Flamed filet mignon." I put said filets on the skillet and it sizzled as it made contact. I put another skillet on, sprinkled it with oil, and turned the heat up. "With potato gratin and pan-fried asparagus." I took a peek inside the oven, where the potato gratin was cooking nicely.

"Flamed?"

"Give them ten minutes and I'll show you."

I chopped up the asparagus quickly, dropped them into their skillet, and then felt the filets. A couple more minutes should do it.

"I've never tasted asparagus." He leant against the counter where he could see everything I was doing. "I can't remember a time when I was required to eat vegetables."

I glanced at him, feeling bad for him all over again. Through my entire childhood, I'd always been told to eat all my greens. Maybe that was why I actually liked all kinds of vegetable too. I imagined people who weren't required to eat it, wouldn't develop the taste for all of them.

"They are quite tasty." I turned the filets mignons over.

I heard the shower turn off, which meant Dion would be right out. I stirred the asparagus and had another peek in on the potato gratin.

"Can I help with something?"

"If you could get me three plates, that would be wonderful." I took the potato au gratin out of the oven and put in on the counter to cool off some.

He did as told and I used a spatula to move the ring of potatoes to each their plate. I held the edge of the hot ring, cutting carefully around the potatoes to loosen them.

"You've got four of them," Chad pointed out.

"Yeah, supposed to be two for each of us. But Dion eats more, so he can have two."

Chad started biting down on his lip again. "I'm sorry I ruined your dinner."

"You didn't." I finished with the fourth ring of potato then divided the asparagus. "It's all good."

"What are you making?" Dion came striding into the kitchen, towel rubbing at his short, wet hair. He stopped once he saw Chad, and Chad stilled as well. "You're back."

"Got out early." I could tell Chad tried for a smile, but his apparent nervousness made it fall flat.

Dion wasn't as nervous. He walked straight over to him and hugged him tight.

Chad's arms gripped onto Dion's tee and his face buried against Dion's shoulder.

I took the brandy down from the cupboard, and I had it open and ready before I realised something.

I felt the filets. They were ready to be flambéed,

but brandy was an alcohol beverage, and Chad was supposed to stay away from alcohol. I moved one of the filets over to the skillet I'd used for the asparagus, thankful I hadn't put it in the sink yet.

"I'm going to flambé now."

"Oh!" Chad let go off Dion with such a speed it all seemed a flurry and he came to lean on the counter again so he could see what I was doing.

I removed the skillet from the heat, and poured the brandy. Then I tilted it away from me and lit the alcohol. It flared up, then slowly burned out. I put the filets on two plates, one on mine and two on Dion's, then I took the one I'd put aside on the third plate.

"If I'd known you were coming, I would've planned something else." I gave him an apologetic smile.

"Don't alcohol burn off?" he glanced from me to the skillet.

"People seem to think so, but it doesn't. At least not for the short amount of time it's lit. Flambéing burns off maybe twenty five percent of it, but you're not supposed to have any alcohol so…" I trailed off.

"You remembered." He seemed honestly surprised.

"Well, yeah." How could I not remember such an important piece of information?

Dion smiled at me then he clapped a hand on Chad's thin shoulder. "Let's sit and eat."

We crowded around the small kitchen table, as we didn't have a dining room and sitting on the sofa felt too informal for the fancy food.

"This is good, Jem," Dion complimented the food, making a sound of appreciation.

Chad nodded his head quickly. "It really was. Even the asparagus."

I smiled wryly at him. "Well, it's time to start eating your greens, innit?"

"Never too late to start." Chad smiled to, but he bowed his head so I couldn't keep staring at him. He looked good when he smiled, though, no doubt about it. And with a face that was completely devoid of any swelling or bruises.

"Do you have to go back to the hospital for more treatment or did they let you out for good?" Dion asked Chad.

"Out for good, yeah. But there's this day centre I have to go to in the beginning, as well as I have to keep my appointments with my doctor to check for any side-effects from the medicine. I also have to see a psychiatrist regularly. Maybe even attend group therapy. They liked group therapy in the hospital and they recommended I continue with it."

Dion nodded. "If you feel it helps, then that's great."

"I don't know." He shrugged. "Loads of strangers listening to my problems? Not so sure about it."

"Strangers that may have the same problems as you. Were there only bipolar people in group therapy?"

"No, there was a mix of things. One had schizophrenia, one was suicidal… There was a variety, but a couple of them were bipolar, yeah."

"Did they have the same symptoms as you?" I asked once I'd swallowed a piece of the filet mignon. It was so tender it almost melted on my tongue.

"Do they see stars and hear their mother's voice?" He snorted. "No. One of them only had bipolar two, which doesn't have mania and psychosis. The other has psychosis, but he had grandiose delusions. Religious ones."

"You had those?"

Another snort. "Not religious ones, no. Thankfully. If I thought I was Jesus or God or the Holy Spirit, I don't know what I would've done."

We fell into silence for a couple of minutes while we ate. I didn't know what to say, and I reckoned they didn't either.

Once we finished dinner, we relocated to the living room, leaving the dishes to do later. Chad claimed the smaller sofa, while Dion and I sat reasonably far apart on the bigger one.

"What're your plans ahead, Chad?" Dion spoke up eventually.

He looked like a deer caught in headlight all of a sudden. "I don't know."

"You want to go back to college in the autumn?"

Good question.

If Chad stayed with us and went back to finish his education... that would be a problem.

"I don't know," he muttered again, fiddling with a small hole in his jeans. "Harriet said I could get day shifts at the Café. Late shifts too, if I was up for it, but mainly day shifts as that's when she's there alone. I think I might just do that until I figure out what else I want to do."

"That sounds like a good plan," I interjected, because it did. He needed to focus on himself, on getting better. Having a few shifts a week would help keep his mind busy, but I wasn't sure college would be a good thing until he found his feet back in the real world. It was taxing going to college, to study for your A-levels, the pressure was high.

He lifted his head to look at me. "She also said you were interested in taking shifts in the kitchen."

Dion's head swivelled to me now. "You are?"

"Yeah, well, she mentioned she needed some help,

and it's not like I'm attached to my current job. It would be a lot better to work there, than the shitty place I'm in now. It's still not a high-class restaurant like my previous job, but at least I feel like I can stand to stay in that job while I look for something more challenging."

"Okay, yeah, I see your point." He turned back to Chad. "Have you heard anything more about Wynn?"

"Still in hospital. I went over there before I came here, which is why I was so late. But they wouldn't let me in. They did say he's doing fine though, so I guess that's something." He was back to fiddling with the hole in his jeans.

My eyes were drawn to his bag, still lying where he'd dropped it close to the door. "You should unpack," I said, offering him the out to answering anymore questions. He seemed like he needed some time to himself.

"Oh." His head turned to where my gaze was locked. "Yeah." He stood and shuffled over to lift the bag up, and with one final insecure glance our way, he slipped into the guest-room.

Dion drummed his fingers on his thigh. "We didn't speak about this."

"Hmm?"

"About the space. We haven't got any closet space

in our room, only the guest room, but if he's got all his stuff in the guest-room, won't he feel like a guest?"

"I think…" What did I think? I had no idea. "Maybe him staying in the guest room is best for now? I mean, we don't know what's going to happen. Maybe a lot, maybe nothing. Maybe he'll feel comfortable in the guest room? You really think he'll feel bad about it?" I didn't want him to feel bad or unwelcome, because he *was* welcome.

"I'll go have a chat with him." Dion pushed himself up and headed over to the room in question. He left the door open, but from the position I was in, I couldn't see either of them. All I could hear was muffled voices.

I decided that conversation was best had between the two of them.

They were the ones with the connection after all, so I stood to do the dishes. It didn't take me terribly long to rinse the plates off and put in the dishwasher, or clean out the skillets I'd used.

When I entered the living room again, I had a direct line of sight to the two of them, still in the guest room.

And kissing.

Chad's head was tilted up, Dion's neck was bent a

bit, and their lips slid together softly. Both had their eyes closed.

I felt like a voyeur, so I ducked my head and headed back over to the sofa where I couldn't see them.

I could still see them in my mind though. Part of me didn't like that my boyfriend was kissing someone else, but that part wasn't all that big anymore. The other part kind of thought it'd been a hot sight, the two of them together. And as long as that was the biggest part, I suppose we'd be okay.

Hopefully, anyway.

Dion came out of the bedroom, a bit of guilt on his face.

"I thought it was hot," I told him, not wanting him to feel guilty for something I'd suggested in the first place.

He startled. "What was?"

"The two of you. Kissing."

"Oh." He smiled slightly, embarrassed. "I think you should go talk to him."

"What for?" I blinked up at him.

"To just reassure him. I don't think I managed to. He knows I want him here, but he's unsure if you're being truthful or not."

"Right." It was my turn to push myself up. Dion

took his old place back as I headed over to knock on the door, which was still slightly open.

Chad turned from where he was folding a pair of jeans on the bed.

"You'll be okay in here?" I stepped inside and slid the door half-closed.

"Yeah. It's great."

"Dion says you don't believe I want you here." I leant against the wall, not wanting to crowd him.

"I can't imagine you wanting to. I mean, you know how I feel about him, and I made him cheat on you and your relationship wasn't doing so well afterwards."

"But it's doing okay now." I kept my gaze resting on him, while he in turn didn't seem to be able to look at me. "Dion told you what we'd been talking about, two weeks ago when you were in hospital. What I proposed."

"You still want that?" He gave me a leery look.

"I do, yes. I think… I don't know. I think it might be good. A good thing." I crossed my arms self-consciously. "But I also think we should take it slow. We don't know each other. You know Dion as your teacher, first and foremost, but you still know him better than you know me. I don't think we should rush anything, because that could only lead to things getting worse. Slow is right, at least in my opinion."

TT KOVE

He nodded slowly, finally turning to face me fully. "I would really like to get to know you."

"Yeah?" My heart started beating faster by that simple admission. "Me too. To know you, I mean."

A smile spread slowly on his lips. He quelled it by biting down on his lower lip, but it was still impossible to hide. It was full of hope and that realisation hit me like a hammer to the chest.

"Want to go back out?" I motioned my head towards the door. "It's still early. We'll just chill on the sofa and watch some telly. A normal night in this flat."

He nodded and walked over to me. There was a moment of hesitation, and then he hugged me. "Thanks," he murmured, then quickly slid past me to head towards the door.

I followed close on his heels.

Dion looked up at us from where he still sat on the sofa, in the same spot. "You all right?" His gaze flicked from one of us to the other.

"Yeah," I said with conviction. "Yeah, we're fine."

And I really did think we would be, eventually.

ABOUT THE AUTHOR

TT lives in Norway and writes about gay men living in Norway. She also occasionally writes about gay men living in the UK, because she loves the UK. Norway might be too cold for her, but TT doesn't like the summer, so she's learned to adapt. TT is happiest in front of her computer, creating emotional stories about men loving other men.

www.ttkove.com
ttkove@gmail.com

www.ingramcontent.com/pod-product-compliance
Lightning Source LLC
Chambersburg PA
CBHW032136190626
46814CB00005BA/1718